"Would you like that?" he asked, leaning into her, his smoldering gaze probing and intense. "Would you like to feel my hands all over your body?"

You have no idea.

Electricity crackled between them, caused the air in the room to swelter. Nicco seized Jariah around the waist and drew her right up to his chest. Then the unthinkable happened—he kissed her. He brushed his lips against her mouth, gently at first, but the kiss quickly evolved into a passionate, desperate plea. Nicco kissed her with urgency, with a passionate, ferocious heat.

They'd crossed the line, jumped headfirst over it, and now there was no turning back.

Burying her hands in his hair, Jariah grabbed a fistful of curls and stirred her fingers around his dark, lush locks. Playing in his hair increased her desire, her sexual hunger. Finally, after weeks of stolen glances and lascivious smiles she knew just how delicious his mouth tasted. And it was better than she'd imagined. Beyond her wildest dreams. His lips were flavored with wine, carried a hint of spice, and the intoxicating blend made her delirious with need.

For a split second, Jariah considered fleeing the private tasting room, but she was helpless to resist his kiss, and his sweet, sensuous caress.

Books by Pamela Yaye

Harlequin Kimani Romance

Other People's Business
The Trouble with Luv'
Her Kind of Man
Love TKO
Games of the Heart
Love on the Rocks
Pleasure for Two
Promises We Make
Escape to Paradise
Evidence of Desire
Passion by the Book
Designed by Desire
Seduced by the Playboy
Seduced by the CEO

PAMELA YAYE

has a bachelor's degree in Christian education. Her love for African-American fiction prompted her to pursue a career in writing romance. When she's not working on her latest novel, this busy wife, mother and teacher is watching basketball, cooking or planning her next vacation. Pamela lives in Alberta, Canada, with her gorgeous husband and adorable, but mischievous, son and daughter.

Seduced
BY THE CEO

Pamela Yaye

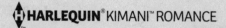

HARLEQUIN® KIMANI™ ROMANCE

This book is dedicated to single mothers everywhere. I hope you find a sexy, romantic man like Nicco Morretti who sweeps you off your feet and cherishes you every day of your life. I wrote this one for you moms, so enjoy!!!

Recycling programs for this product may not exist in your area.

ISBN-13: 978-0-373-86366-2

SEDUCED BY THE CEO

Copyright © 2014 by Pamela Sadadi

Printed in U.S.A.

Dear Reader,

I'm going to let you in on a little secret: I like bad boys *a lot*. I love their swag, their confidence, how they own every room they enter and even their wild, adventurous side. That's why I had a blast writing Nicco Morretti's story. The celebrated restaurateur is one of the most captivating men you'll ever meet, and the moment I put my pen to the paper his story consumed me. The CEO with the model good looks has it all: smarts, charisma *and* sizzling sex appeal, but a chance meeting with single mom Jariah Brooks forces Nicco to rethink his bad-boy ways.

Jariah doesn't believe in mixing business with pleasure, and indulging in a tawdry office romance with her bad-boy boss would be career suicide. Besides, the Italian heartthrob is all wrong for her. He's arrogant and flashy, everything *she* doesn't want in a man, but after a magical first kiss, she realizes there's more to Nicco than meets the eye. They're destined to be together, and although the odds—*and* his mother—are against them, Nicco is determined to make Jariah his one and only.

Seduced by the Heir, featuring Nicco's big brother, Rafael Morretti, hits shelves soon.

I would LOVE to hear from you, so drop me a line at pamelayaye@aol.com, find me on Facebook or visit my website, www.pamelayaye.com. Thanks for the support. Happy reading, and be blessed.

With love,

Pamela Yaye

Chapter 1

Famed restaurateur, Nicco Morretti, watched celebrity party planner Claudia Jefferies-Medina sail through the doors of Javalicious and noted that as usual, she was right on time. Smiling broadly, he stood and pulled out a chair for her at their table. Celebrating the grand reopening of his restaurant lounge, Dolce Vita, last night left Nicco feeling sluggish. But he quickly shook off his fatigue and smiled. "Good morning, Claudia."

"It's great to see you again." Kissing him on both cheeks, Claudia greeted him as if they'd known each other all of their lives rather than just a month.

"Thanks for agreeing to meet me on such short notice. I really appreciate it."

"No problem," Claudia said as she sat down, took off her white blazer and draped it behind her chair. "I was already in town on business, so squeezing you in this morning was a cinch."

"I ordered you a cappuccino when the waiter came by earlier. I hope that's okay."

"You remembered what kind of coffee I like," she said,

touching a hand to her chest. "Thank you, Nicco. That was very thoughtful of you."

The waiter arrived, tray in hand, and placed two steaming mugs on the round wooden table. "Would you like to order something from the breakfast menu?"

"Nothing for me," Nicco said, reaching for his coffee mug. "I'm good."

While Claudia chatted with the waiter about the morning specials, Nicco studied the thin, long-haired women seated beside the front window. They grinned lasciviously, and he did, too, making a mental note to introduce himself to the blond babes after his meeting with Claudia ended. He glanced around the sparsely decorated café, surprised to see that it was filled to capacity. The quaint coffee shop attracted locals and tourists alike, and although it was only nine o'clock in the morning, a steady stream of casually dressed people shuffled through the open door. The scent of sea water mingled with the aromas wafting around the café, and the sound of squawking birds and laughter filled the air.

"Have you had a chance to review the notes I sent you last week?"

Nicco wanted to laugh, but didn't. Claudia sat on the edge of her seat, her eyes bright and her excitement sky high. "I think my mom will get a kick out of the live band, and the vintage photo booth, but the rest of the report didn't wow me."

Claudia frowned as if confused by his words, but she didn't speak.

"The party's too small, too low-key. It needs to be grand, flashy and over-the-top."

"Nicco, it doesn't get much bigger than the grand ballroom at the Biltmore Hotel," she said, sounding as animated as a high school cheerleader. "I've done several events at the Biltmore, and they outdo themselves every single time. If you'd like, I could email you some pictures of the pre-Grammy party I did back in January."

Nicco shook his head. "That won't be necessary."

"Are you sure? I think if you saw some pictures you'd feel differently about us booking the Biltmore. It's a gorgeous hotel rich in history and culture, and one of my personal favorites."

"I'm just not feeling it, Claudia, so please keep searching for another venue." His mind was made up. Nicco tasted his coffee, and leaned back comfortably in his chair. He loved the Biltmore Hotel, and thought the food and service was outstanding. But he didn't want to have his parents' anniversary party in a hotel where he'd had numerous sexual liaisons. But he couldn't tell Claudia that, not without looking like a sleaze ball. He wanted the celebrity party planner to think he was a mature, upstanding guy. So, spilling the beans about his past escapades at the historic hotel was definitely out of the question. "My parents worked hard to give me and my brothers a great life in this country, and I want to throw them the most expensive, outrageous anniversary bash Miami has ever seen!"

Claudia was silent for a moment. "What about a mega yacht?"

"Will three hundred people fit comfortably inside?"

"When did the guest list balloon to three hundred people?" she asked, raising an eyebrow.

"Once word got out that my parents were celebrating their twenty-fifth wedding anniversary, our relatives in Venice and Florence insisted on making the trip to Miami."

"The more the merrier, right?"

"That's the Morretti way!"

"Trust me, it's the Mexican way, too. A small family dinner at my in-laws' place usually involves hundreds of people, and more food and alcohol than a Carnival Cruise ship!" Claudia laughed out loud, but quickly sobered and continued her spiel. "A mega yacht can comfortably hold up to five hundred people, and has everything you can think of—lavish staterooms, a lounge, a formal dining room, a pool and even a personal theater. You name it, the yacht's got it."

"Interesting," Nicco said, stroking the length of his jaw. "That could work."

"I'll look into it and get back to you once I find out more information. Can I get your assistant's new number?" she asked, her pen poised to write. "I rang her yesterday to confirm our meeting this morning, but her cell phone has been disconnected."

"Gracie no longer works for Morretti Inc."

"That's too bad. I really liked Ms. O'Connor. Have you found a replacement yet?"

"No, but my HR director is in the process of interviewing suitable candidates as we speak." Nicco raised his mug to his lips and took a swig of coffee. "Hopefully she'll find someone soon, but in the meantime you can reach me by phone or email."

"That works for me."

"One last thing. I want the party to be a surprise, so I'd appreciate if you kept everything quiet." Leaning forward in his chair, he glanced conspicuously around the café to ensure no one was listening in. "The only people who know about the anniversary bash are my brothers, Demetri and Rafael, and I'd like to keep it that way."

"I can do that!" She fervently nodded her head. "Covert is my middle name!"

Laughing, they clinked coffee mugs.

Claudia's cell phone vibrated, and when she glanced at the screen, her face brightened. "I apologize for the interruption," she said, swiping her cell phone off the table. "Do you mind if I take this call? It's my husband, and I'm worried he's still stuck at the Orlando airport."

"Please, by all means, go ahead."

Claudia pressed her cell phone to her ear. *"Santiago, bebé, ¿estás bien?"*

For the second time in minutes, Nicco swallowed a laugh. Claudia sounded more like a love-struck teenager, than an accomplished businesswoman who'd recently been featured in top magazines. With her cell phone at her ear, she swept through the café, speaking in a hushed tone. Nicco scoured the café for the blonds in the daisy dukes he'd spotted earlier, but couldn't find them anywhere. And that sucked, because he needed a woman in his bed *bad*. Like yesterday. Sex was his favorite pastime, the only thing ever worth missing a round of golf with his brothers for. And Nicco couldn't think of anything better than having a gorgeous woman—or two—between his black satin sheets.

Punching in his cell phone password, he fired off a quick text to his older brother, Rafael, and waited anxiously for his reply. For months, Nicco had been debating whether or not to buy Javalicious, and as he sat in his corner table watching the staff fly around the room like busy bees, he decided investing in the coffee shop would be a smart, solid business move. And if Rafael agreed, he'd be one step closer to owning the popular Ocean Drive café just steps away from Miami Beach.

"Wesley, I don't need you to take care of me. I'm a strong, intelligent woman who can take care of herself. Got it?"

Frowning, Nicco shot a glance over his shoulder, curious to see who was responsible for the loud, angry outburst. Seated directly behind him, a woman with short black hair and dressed in pink workout gear spoke on her cell phone. Nicco couldn't see her face, but there was no mistaking her frustration, or the contempt in her voice for the person on the line.

"Please, you wouldn't know the truth if it walked up and slapped you!"

Nicco cracked up. But when he saw the puzzled expressions on the faces of the patrons seated nearby, he killed his laughter and pretended to read the menu card propped up against the napkin holder.

"Sorry about that." Claudia took her seat and rested her cell phone on the table. "My husband was calling to give me an update on his schedule. He'll be in Miami within the hour."

"Then don't let me keep you," Nicco said. "We're finished, so go meet your husband."

"Are you sure?"

"I'm positive."

Up on her feet, her eyes twinkling like diamonds, she collected her things and flashed a friendly wave. "Take care of yourself, Nicco. I'll be in touch."

The second Claudia rushed out the café doors, Nicco searched the room for the woman in the pink workout gear. He found her standing in line, typing furiously on her cell phone, wearing a cheeky grin. Nicco stood in the middle of the café, staring at her. Her facial features were perfect, and so was her taut derriere. Last night, at the grand reopening of Dolce Vita, he'd met scores of women, but they all looked the same—long, silky hair, coats of thick makeup, wearing tiny dresses that left nothing to the imagination. But the woman in front of him now with the killer curves and big brown eyes instantly seized his attention. *She's a stunner, nothing short of magnificent, the most striking woman on the face of the earth.*

Nicco moved forward, toward her. Couldn't help it. Couldn't stop himself. His hands itched to touch her, to squeeze, to caress and stroke her delectable, hourglass shape. Her tank top showed off toned arms, her leggings fit her body like a second skin, and her neon-pink sneakers drew his gaze down the length of her long, sculptured legs.

God bless the man who invented spandex! The woman had a body that made him salivate. Her looks were jaw-dropping, clear off the Richter scale, and Nicco found it impossible to turn away from her. He more than liked what he saw—her dimpled cheeks, the beauty mark above her mouth and most importantly her fine, feminine figure. His thoughts were all over the place, jumping from one illicit image to the next. Battling the needs of his flesh, he stood transfixed, unable to move.

The woman glanced up from her cell phone and caught his eye. Nicco's heart rate sped up, beating at a wild, fanatic pace. For a moment, all he could do was stare helplessly at the beauty standing across the room. That's it. Breathing required every single drop of energy he had left.

Her glossy, pink lips slowly curled into a smile, one that hit him straight in the heart. And when his eyes zeroed in on her moist, lush mouth, Nicco imagined himself planting one on her. A long, sensuous kiss that would turn her on.

Nicco watched the woman pay her bill, and when she headed in his direction, he surfaced from his sexual haze. Clearing his throat, he racked his brain for the right pick-up line, one that would capture her attention and buy him a few precious minutes of her time.

"How was your workout?" Nicco winced when he heard the question slide past his lips.

How was your workout? mocked his inner voice. *Surely you can do better than that. Quit staring at her cleavage, man, and get your head in the game!*

Her feet slowed and a frown bruised her lips. "My workout?" she repeated, regarding him closely. "Were you in my Bootie Camp class this morning?"

Nicco chuckled. "No, unfortunately I missed it. Where do you teach?"

"Why? Are you looking to drop a few pounds?"

"Do I need to?" Raising an eyebrow, he cocked his head to the right. Nicco wanted her to get a good look at him, so he stood tall and squared his shoulders. He saw her eyelashes widen and flutter, and heard her quick intake of breath. She darted a glance down at his shoes and a sly grin claimed his mouth. *That's right, baby. I wear a size twelve shoe. How you like me now?*

"Since you're a fitness instructor, I'd love your expert opinion." Nicco rested his hands on his waist and displayed a bold, in-your-face stance. "Am I in good shape or not?"

Rolling her eyes, an exasperated expression marring her features, she heaved her gym bag over her shoulder and stepped past him as if he hadn't just asked her a question.

Nicco didn't know what possessed him to touch her, but when his hands connected with her flesh he felt a rush, a charge so powerful his knees buckled. They stood in the middle of the café, staring at each other. His desire for her so strong, his mind went blank. "Please don't go. We're not finished talking."

Leaning forward, he read the name printed on the top hand corner of her tank top. *Jariah Brooks.* Nicco tried it on for size, allowing the syllables to stroke the length of his tongue, before deciding that her name was as striking as her dark, creamy complexion. "I'd love to take you out sometime, Jariah. Can I get your phone number?"

"I'm busy."

"Every night?"

"Look," she snapped, "I'm having a really bad day, and I'm not in the mood to hear any of your slick lines, so go hit on someone else."

"Let's sit down and talk."

"Let's not and say we did."

"Do you know who I am?"

Jariah sputtered a laugh. "No, should I?"

"I think so." Bragging was usually beneath him, but to impress the saucy fitness instructor, he was willing to use every trick in the book. "I'm well-known around these parts. My picture is always in the newspapers and on TV."

She stared at him for a moment, as if trying to place his face, then fervently nodded her head. "Oh, wow," she gushed, pointing a finger at him. "I thought you looked familiar."

A grin overwhelmed Nicco's mouth. Finally. Now that Jariah recognized him—and knew that he was one of the most successful restaurateurs in the nation—they could skip the preamble and head straight to the penthouse suite at his favorite, luxury hotel. He had plans for Jariah, plans that involved whip cream, Cristal, and a box of Magnum condoms, and the sooner they got to his suite at the Hilton Bentley the better.

"You were on last night's episode of *Cheaters,* weren't you?"

Hanging his head, Nicco clutched his shirt, as if wounded by the dig, but deep down he was amused. Aroused actually. He loved their playful banter. Much like her stunning looks, Jariah's cheeky wit was a turn-on. But what Nicco liked most about the mocha-brown was her mouth. Her lips were thick, moist and plump, and looked incredibly inviting.

"Sorry, but I'm not interested."

"Not interested?" Nicco chuckled a laugh. "Can't say I've ever heard *that* one before."

"There's a first time for everything," she said in a sing-song voice.

"Are you married?"

"Why?" she quipped. "Are you looking for your *one true love?*"

Nicco choked on his tongue. *Hell, no!* he thought, sliding his hands into the back pocket of his blue Levi's jeans.

I'm only thirty-four and besides I'm far too smart to ever do something as stupid as tying the knot! Nicco caught himself, just as he felt a tidal wave of guilt. Not everyone who fell in love and got married was foolish. His kid brother, Demetri, had found love with news reporter Angela Kelly—and he'd never seen a happier, more loving couple. Since popping the question last month on live TV, Demetri and Angela had become the newest celebrity "it" couple, and every time Nicco talked to his brother he waxed poetic about his new fiancée and their upcoming wedding.

Happily ever after isn't for everyone, and it certainly isn't for me. Nicco didn't do relationships, and rarely saw the same woman twice, but he was willing to make an exception for Jariah-Curves-Galore-Brooks. One night with the saucy beauty wouldn't be enough. He'd need a week with her, shoot, maybe even two or three.

Nicco couldn't think straight. It was hard for him to stay present in the moment. He felt unsteady on his feet, as if he'd been smacked upside the head by a Roger Clemons fastball. This had never happened to him before. Ever. No one had ever affected him like this. Over the years he'd hooked up with a wide assortment of red-carpet darlings, but Jariah Brooks was the first and only woman to ever take his breath away.

His heart roared like the engine of his Harley Davidson, and when Jariah moistened her lips with her tongue, Nicco strangled a groan. *I don't know how much more of this I can take,* he thought, raking a hand through his short, curly hair.

"Mommy!"

Nicco felt someone bump the back of his legs and a cold liquid splash onto his sandals. A chubby, wide-eyed girl with pigtails jumped into Jariah's arms and giggled with delight. Her hands swung wildly, and every time she moved her drink splashed onto him.

Stepping back, Nicco snatched a wad of napkins off the breakfast counter along the front window and dabbed at the front of his black V-neck T-shirt.

"Mommy, can we go to the beach? Please? Pretty please?" the girl whined, tugging on her mother's tank top. "I promise to be a good listener."

"Not today, Ava. You have a dentist appointment at ten forty-five."

The girl stamped her foot. "But I don't want to go to the stinky dentist. I want to go to the beach! You promised I could go swimming!"

Intrigued by the exchange, Nicco glanced up. The little girl was the splitting image of Jariah. Mother and daughter shared the same dark brown complexion, wide, expressive eyes, and delicate button nose. A tanned, stocky man joined them, and kissed Jariah on each cheek. He wore a lopsided smile, and was so smitten with the fitness instructor he had stars in his eyes.

Feeling dumb for hitting on her, Nicco mentally berated himself for publicly making a fool of himself. He watched the trio exit the café, and as Jariah strode past the front window, hand-in-hand with her daughter, their eyes met. She caught him staring at her—again—but this time Nicco didn't flash his trademark grin. There was nothing to smile about. Jariah had a kid, and at least *two* men in her life. And since children and drama were a turn-off Nicco tore his gaze away from her pretty face and studied his diamond Montblanc wristwatch instead.

Nicco dumped his napkins in the garbage. He had to hurry or he'd be late. He had an eleven o'clock meeting with the head of his security team, Gerald Stanley, and was anxious to hear if the former navy SEAL had garnered any new information about the break-in at his downtown restaurant. The perpetrators had caused thousands of dollars' worth of damage, but two months later the police still had no leads. He suspected deep in his gut that his ex-assistant, Gracie O'Connor, was involved, but he wasn't ready to share his thoughts with anyone. He was going to handle it his way, and no one was going to stop him—not even his brothers.

How had things come to this? How had things gone so bad, so quickly? Nicco wondered, expelling a deep, troubled breath. A year ago, he'd been on top of the world, living the good life, but the day before his thirty-fourth birthday his whole world had fallen apart. Twelve months later, he was still picking up the pieces.

Slipping on his aviator sunglasses, he strode purposefully through the café doors. Outside, at the intersection of Ocean Drive and First Street, Nicco spotted Jariah and her daughter. The little girl was cute, every bit as beautiful as her mother, and Nicco couldn't help thinking what a great-looking family they were.

Nicco shook his head, dismissed the unsolicited thought that rose in his mind. *Jariah Brooks is a stunner, but I definitely dodged a bullet there.* Kids weren't his thing, but playing the field definitely was, and as soon as he finished his workday he was making a move on the full-figured brunette at his favorite spa. The masseuse wasn't as witty as Jariah Brooks was, but she was the ready, willing, down-for-whatever-in-the-bedroom type, and tonight, that was all that mattered to Nicco Morretti.

Chapter 2

Jariah sat at the conference room table inside Morretti Inc. mentally preparing for her interview. Her heart was beating so loud and fast she feared she would collapse. As Jariah waited for the Human Resources Director to arrive, she straightened her dress and assessed her look. Jariah was excited about the account manager position, but worried her nerves would get the best of her and she'd trip all over her words.

Glancing around the conference room, she took in the tasteful paintings, the leafy plants positioned beside the window and the low-hanging lights. *I have to nail this interview. I need this job and the salary even more.* Jariah had been out of work for months, and pounding the pavement had yet to produce any results. Teaching aerobic classes at Premier Fitness was great fun, and she loved seeing her students' progress each week, but the paycheck just wasn't cutting it. Her bills were piling up, and Jariah feared if she didn't land a full-time position soon she'd have to dip into her emergency fund.

And what will I do once that *runs out?* Jariah told herself not to imagine the worst possible scenario—the one with her losing her home and crawling back to her ex-fiancé. It didn't matter what Wesley said. She *would* make it without him, and when she did, she'd finally be able to give her daughter, Ava, the life she'd always dreamed of. And she didn't need Wesley or anyone else to help make it happen.

Turning her face toward the window, she closed her eyes and allowed the sunshine raining down from the morning sky to calm her fears. Jariah felt herself relax, felt the tension radiating through her cold, chilled body recede. Hearing her cell phone vibrate from inside her purse, Jariah slid a hand into the side pocket and took out her Black-Berry. Jariah had three new text messages from Wesley, and each one was more annoying than the last. He was furious that she had refused to get back together with him. So he'd been blowing up her phone for weeks, his cruel taunts only proved how immature he was.

Switching off her cell phone, she dropped it inside her purse, and sat back comfortably in her leather wingback chair. Jariah was sick of Wesley's superior, know-it-all attitude and she refused to take any of his calls.

Wesley Covington, the twenty-nine-year-old chief administrative deputy making waves from Orange County to Capitol Hill, was not only the father of her daughter, but an overgrown child himself. The Ivy League graduate had the power to ruin a perfectly good day, and as Jariah thought about the messages he'd sent her, she wondered for the umpteenth time what she'd ever seen in the privileged mama's boy.

Why can't I meet a nice guy? Jariah wondered, releasing a troubled sigh. Someone sweet, chivalrous and romantic, who was good with kids. Hoping the man upstairs was listening, she stared up at the ceiling pitifully, as if that would seal the deal. *A little chemistry would be nice, too,* she thought with a fervent nod of her head. Since calling it quits with Wesley eight months ago, Jariah had been on dozens of dates but none of the guys she met excited her.

A picture of a tall, gorgeous guy with intense eyes and curly hair sprang in her mind. As Jariah sat there, thinking about the hottie who'd approached her at Javalicious on Friday, she inwardly chastised herself for not giving him her phone number. *Why?* her inner voice questioned. *He's a player who's probably bedded more women than Hugh Hefner!*

Hearing a sharp knock on the door, she shot to her feet and adjusted her Donna Karen dress. The door opened, and Jariah stood there, dumbfounded. Her lips parted, but nothing came out. *What the hell? What is he doing here?* It was the guy from Javalicious. The one who'd hit on her, and probably every other woman in the popular café. On Friday, he'd looked handsome in his casual T-shirt and khaki pants, but today he looked like a Hugo Boss model fresh off the runway. Clean-cut, with thick eyebrows, and sideburns, his ebony-black hair a mass of short, tight curls, he carried himself like a man who was used to getting his way in the boardroom *and* in the bedroom. All arms and legs, he was the height of a basketball player, and had the strong, muscled physique to match.

Her eyes slid greedily down his chiseled body. His shoulders filled out every inch of his lightweight suit jacket, his sky-blue shirt showed off the powerful definition of his upper chest, and his tailored pants hung just so. The man knew how to rock a suit, and smelled as debonair as he looked. He was cool, suave and hot—just like she remembered. He wasn't the kind of man a woman forgot, and as he crossed the room toward her, Jariah felt a rush of panic. Her palms grew slick with sweat, and if her knees shook any harder her legs would give way.

"We meet again," the stranger said in a velvety smooth voice. "Jariah, right?"

Taken by his smile and his dreamy scent, all Jariah could do was nod her head. *Is this really happening?* she wondered. *Am I actually standing face-to-face with the guy I blew off two days ago?* He was too close, but Jariah didn't move. Couldn't, not when he was openly staring at her. The Italian hunk was the sexiest thing on two legs, but something about him still rubbed her the wrong way. Jariah didn't know anything about the attractive stranger, but she could spot a player a mile away, and this guy was definitely that. His cocksure stance said it all: I'm handsome and charming and I can have any woman I want.

Not me Casanova, so back off!

"I thought that was you. I glanced into the conference room, and there you were." He slid a hand casually into his pocket, stood there as if he had all the time in the world to shoot the breeze. "Shouldn't you be at the gym teaching the morning Bootie Camp class?"

"Are you stalking me?"

His eyes gleamed with mischief. "No. Would you like me to?"

Jariah couldn't think of a witty comeback to put him in his place, so she said nothing.

"I'm just kidding," he said, holding his hands up in the air, as if he was surrendering to Miami's finest. "I work here. What's your story?"

"If you must know, I'm here for a job interview."

"That's *really* great news."

Baffled by his statement and his enthusiasm, she said, "It is?"

"Absolutely. This place is filled with a bunch of boring, stuffy suits, and it'll be a nice to have a woman like you around for a change."

"A woman like me?" she repeated, raising an eyebrow. "What is that supposed to mean?"

"You've got moxie, and I find your honesty refreshing."

"You don't know me."

"Not yet," he shot back. "But I'm working on it."

He smelled of expensive cologne, and when he raked a hand through his hair, Jariah wondered what it would be like to play in his dark, thick curls.

"How's your daughter? Did everything go okay at the dentist on Friday?"

Stunned by the question, Jariah eyed him closely, trying to recall their previous conversation. *What is this guy up to? Is it possible that he is stalking me?* He didn't give off that creepy, peeping-tom vibe, but he made her nervous. His questions put her on edge, made her uncomfortable. Before she could put him in his place, the door opened and a skinny brunette wearing designer eyeglasses and a stylish gray pantsuit marched briskly inside.

Stopping abruptly, she said, "Good morning, Mr. Morretti. Is there a problem?"

Jariah didn't hear the gasp that escaped her lips, but it must have shot out of her mouth in surround-sound because the brunette gave her a funny look.

Touching a hand to her scalding-hot cheeks, Jariah choked down the lump in the back of her throat. *This young, ridiculously hot guy owns Morretti Incorporated?* Hell, no. No way. It couldn't be, she argued, refusing to believe it. He was the boss's son. Had to be. Remembering their conversation on Friday made Jariah wince. *I am so screwed. There's no way I'm getting this job. Not after the way I spoke to him at the coffee shop.*

"Please, Mrs. Reddick, call me Nicco." His eyes were narrowed, as if he was pissed off, but his mouth held a teasing grin. "Save the formalities for Rafael and my father. I'm far more laid-back. Haven't you figured that out by now?"

Jariah wanted to roll her eyes but didn't. The HR director was wearing a wedding ring the size of a jaw breaker, and was likely in her mid-forties, but she giggled like a kid watching *Finding Nemo*.

"Mrs. Reddick, if it's okay with you I'd like to sit in on this interview."

No, it's not okay! Jariah screamed inside in her head. She prayed the brunette would show Nicco Morretti the door, but when he flashed one of his wide, panty-wetting smiles at the HR director, she eagerly nodded her head.

"Of course, by all means." Mrs. Reddick gestured to the conference room table with more flair than a model at the Miami Car Show. "Please, pull up a chair and join us."

"Can I get you something to drink?" Nicco asked, sliding behind Jariah and holding out her chair. "Coffee? Tea? A glass of wine?"

Jariah felt the compulsion to laugh, but didn't. *Who drinks wine at nine-thirty in the morning?* she wondered. *I bet he does!* Nicco was testing her, but Jariah refused to let the hot-shot businessman unnerve her. Guys like Nicco Morretti—rich, arrogant, womanizers—were a dime a dozen in Miami and hardly her type. It didn't matter that he had dashing good looks, or more swagger than a championship winning bull fighter. He was just a man, and like her ex, not someone she could ever trust. Nicco Morretti was a charmer, a guy who got off on seducing women and no one could tell her otherwise. "No, thank you. I'm fine."

Girl, you better lick those lips and hike up that skirt!

Jariah was appalled by the thought that entered her mind. Yes, Nicco Morretti was attractive, and flirting with him certainly wouldn't hurt her cause, but Jariah wanted to the get the account manager's job on her own merit. Not because she'd flashed some cleavage at the boss's son. She wouldn't do it. No way, no how.

All business, the HR Director sat down with a flourish and opened the manila file folder she'd put down on the round, mahogany table. "Welcome to Morretti Inc., Ms. Brooks. I'm Mrs. Reddick. It's a pleasure to meet you."

To conceal the fact that she was shaking, Jariah crossed her legs, and clasped her hands around her knees. Taking a deep breath didn't calm her nerves, and Jariah feared if she tried to speak nothing would come out.

"Tell us about yourself, Ms. Brooks. What would you like us to know about you?"

Releasing the breath she'd been holding, she sat up straighter in her chair. This was her time to shine, to prove that there was more to her than met the eye, and Jariah held nothing back. She told the HR director about her education, her past work experience, and the joy she found in volunteering with the Meals on Wheels program.

"What makes you stand out from your peers?" Mrs. Reddick asked.

"I'm dependable, trustworthy and responsible. I take great pride in my work, and I'm committed to being the best account manager I can be."

The HR director continued. "What's your worst character trait?"

That depends on who you ask. My parents think I'm irresponsible, my ex says I'm unreasonable, and his mother is convinced I got pregnant to trap her beloved son. The accusation stung, even after all these years, but Jariah didn't have time to dwell on her troubled thoughts. "I can be stubborn at times, especially when I'm very passionate about a project, but I've never allowed my shortcomings to interfere with my ability to do my job."

Mrs. Reddick folded her arms rigidly across her chest, and Jariah knew she'd said the wrong thing, but before she could revise her response, the HR director spoke.

"Why should we hire you, Ms. Brooks?"

"Because I'm a dedicated, hard-working professional who thrives under pressure."

Seduced by the CEO

"Mrs. Reddick, if it's all right with you I'd like to ask Ms. Brooks a few questions."

Bewildered by Nicco Morretti's request, Jariah regarded him coolly. *This isn't good,* she thought as her heart rate sped up.

"Go ahead, Nicco." Mrs. Reddick flapped her hands like a bald eagle taking flight. "She's all yours."

Leaning forward in his chair, his eyes zeroing in on hers, he was nothing like the sly, flirtatious guy who'd hit on her two days earlier. "Why do you want to work for Morretti Inc.?"

Because I'm an out-of-work single mom, and kids are expensive! Unsure of what to say, Jariah racked her mind for a suitable answer, one that would paint her in a favorable light. Over the past three weeks she'd been on so many interviews it was hard to keep the companies straight, and though she tried, Jariah couldn't remember anything remarkable about Morretti Inc. But she couldn't tell the boss's son that, so she said the first thing that came to mind.

"This is not only a fine opportunity for personal growth and professional advancement, but Morretti Inc. is a place where I feel I can make a difference." Hearing the nervous quiver in her voice, Jariah paused to take a deep breath. "As an account manager, well versed in finance, book keeping and stock and investment options, I see this position as a perfect fit for me. Because I have excellent time management skills, I'm able to accomplish a lot in a limited amount of time and I have always led by example."

"Is your significant other supportive of your career ambitions?"

Jariah frowned, and noticed that Mrs. Reddick raised her eyebrows, too. *What an odd question. Is that his way of asking me if I have a boyfriend?* She expected Mrs. Reddick to come to her rescue, but when the HR director didn't, Jariah had no choice but to respond. "I'm single," she said brightly, though she wanted to kick Nicco in the shin for digging around in her personal life. "My daughter is my number one priority right now."

"Do you have any qualms about working at a male-dominated company?"

"Absolutely not. To be honest, I get along better with men than I do with women." The second the words left her mouth Jariah regretted them, but to her surprise, Nicco grinned. He looked amused.

"Do you have any questions for me before we conclude today's interview?"

"Yes, as a matter of fact I do." Jariah held his gaze. For some odd reason seeing the puzzled expression on his face bolstered her courage. "What makes Morretti Inc. different? What sets your company apart from the competition?"

Nicco gave her a long, searching look. "That's a great question, Ms. Brooks."

You impressed the boss's son. You go girl!

"Morretti Inc. has been the leader in the shipping industry for over fifty years, and since expanding our services in the nineties we're increased our profits by 16 percent. In addition to our shipping, moving and security divisions, we also own condominium properties, car dealerships and a wildly successful restaurant franchise. Have you heard of Dolce Vita?"

Yes, but it's too expensive for my tastes. "Yes, of course. It's a celebrity hotspot, and one of my favorite Italian restaurants in Miami."

Jariah fidgeted with her fingers and shifted uncomfortably in her chair. Lying didn't sit well with her. It troubled her conscience, made her feel like a fraud but she felt compelled to tell Nicco Morretti what he wanted to hear. The interview was going well, better than she'd expected, and she didn't want to do anything to turn him off. "Can you tell me about your employee development program?"

Mrs. Reddick spoke up. "We have a mandatory, one-week training session for all new employees, monthly webinars and workshops and a tuition reimbursement program for all full-time employees enrolled in university classes."

"That's impressive," Jariah said, meaning every word. "When will you make a decision about the account manager position?"

"By Wednesday." Mrs. Reddick closed her file folder. "Do you have any other questions?"

Shaking her head, Jariah picked her purse up off the floor and stood to her feet. "Thank you for taking time out of your very busy schedule to meet with me this morning."

"No, thank you for coming." Nicco stood and gestured to the door. "I'll walk you out."

"That won't be necessary. I remember the way."

"If you insist."

"I do."

Stepping forward, Jariah took the hand Nicco offered, and gave it a firm shake. Ignoring the warmth of his touch, she strode through the conference room door with her shoulders squared and her head held high.

Staring through the glass window, Nicco watched Jariah walk down the hallway with the grace of a woman twice her age. Her sleeveless dress, which clung to each sinuous curve of her body, made Nicco wonder if she'd ever been a model. He imagined her naked, with nothing on but her red patent leather pumps, and all but exploded in his boxers.

Jariah Brooks is all wrong for you. His conscience pointed out. *She has a kid, man trouble,* and *a serious attitude problem, remember?* Nicco did, but that didn't stop him from wanting her. Intelligent, assertive women turned him on, and he enjoyed Jariah's strong personality and the way she stood up to him. She was definitely a looker, and he liked that she was single…and available.

"What do you think?"

Remembering that he wasn't alone and that Mrs. Reddick was standing beside him, watching him like a hawk, he turned away from the window and shook off his thoughts. "I think Ms. Brooks would be a great addition to our accounting department, don't you?"

"No, I don't."

"You don't?" Nicco heard the surprise in his voice and coughed to clear his throat. After leaving Javalicious on Friday, Nicco had told himself to forget about Jariah, but the message had failed to reach his brain. All weekend, he'd thought of her and nothing else. Running into her at his office had been a stroke of good luck, and after sitting in on her interview, Nicco was even more intrigued by the single mom with the keen mind and stellar résumé. "I was impressed by her answers and the questions she asked."

"Ms. Brooks is articulate, and obviously intelligent, but I don't want to hire anyone who may cause trouble or disrupt the harmony within the accounting department—"

"And you think Ms. Brooks is trouble?"

Mrs. Reddick shoved her papers back into her manila file folder. "I can't say for sure, but I'd rather not take the chance. And besides, she's a single mother."

"What does that have to do with her ability to do the job?"

"In my thirty years of experience in HR, I've found single moms to be unreliable, undependable, and often too distracted by personal issues to effectively do their job."

"That sounds like discrimination, Mrs. Reddick."

"It's called selective hiring."

Her words troubled him, but Nicco decided not to argue with Mrs. Reddick. The HR director was new to

Morrretti Inc., but his father trusted her wholeheartedly, and he didn't want to say anything to ruffle her feathers. "You're the expert. Do what you think is best," he said with a shrug of his shoulders. "Have you hired a new executive assistant for me?"

"Unfortunately, none of the men I've interviewed yesterday were up to snuff."

Stunned, Nicco stared wide-eyed at the HR director. Was Mrs. Reddick off her rocker? What would ever possess her to hire a dude to be his right hand? "Come again?"

"In light of what happened with Ms. O'Conner, your father thought it was best I hire a male assistant to work alongside you, and I agreed."

"I don't give a damn what my father thinks," Nicco snapped, growing annoyed by her condescending tone. He knew what the HR director was implying, and he didn't like it. "I would prefer working with a woman, so please don't discriminate against female applicants."

"I'll keep your wishes in mind, but I have to do what's right for the company..."

Nicco raked a hand through his hair. It wasn't his fault his former assistant, Gracie O'Conner, had developed feelings for him and caused a scene at the company barbecue. Three days later Gracie quit, and when word had got back to company headquarters about the incident his father, Arturo, had reamed him out in English *and* Italian.

His thoughts slid back to the past. Nicco loved everything about women—their strength, their femininity, the way they smelled and looked and moved. But they were also the most cunning, calculating people on the face of the planet. One night, after too many glasses of Cristal, he'd slept with Gracie. The next morning he'd apologized and made it clear that they could never be more than friends, but like all of the other women in his past she'd foolishly thought she could change him. When that didn't work, she threatened to sue him for sexual harassment. To keep her quiet, and their family name out of the tabloids, his father had quietly paid her off.

The muscles in his jaw tightened. Every time he thought about how Gracie had screwed him over, he burned inside. Why did women view him as their meal ticket?

He didn't want to rock the boat or piss off Mrs. Reddick, but he wasn't sold on having a male executive assistant. He needed someone strong and assertive who spoke her mind. Someone like… A light went off in his head. "I want Ms. Brooks."

Mrs. Reddick gasped. "Excuse me?"

"I want Ms. Brooks to be my new executive assistant."

"But she applied for the account manager job."

"I know, but since you're not hiring her for the position, I'd like her to work for me," he said, keeping his tone casual, despite his growing excitement. "Not only does Ms. Brooks have marketing training, she also has extensive experience working with start-up companies, and I bet she has great ideas on how to trim costs without sacrificing value and quality."

Mrs. Reddick pursed her thin lips. "I've been an HR director for more than three decades," she reminded him. "My gut instinct is that Ms. Brooks isn't the right fit for this company."

Nicco dismissed her words with a shake of his head. For some unexplainable reason, he wanted to help the out-of-work single mom. Other women like Gracie enjoyed living off men, but Jariah was independent and charitable, and he admired her ambition. After reading her curriculum vitae, he felt that she'd be a great addition to the Morretti Inc. family. He didn't care what Mrs. Reddick thought. He was hiring Jariah, and that was that. "With all due respect, Mrs. Reddick, I'm quite capable of hiring my own executive assistant."

"Ms. Brooks is a university graduate, with years of experience working in finance," she said matter-of-factly. "Being an EA is beneath her. She won't take the position."

"She will." Nicco adjusted his tie and flashed a broad grin. "Because I'm going to make Ms. Brooks an offer she can't refuse."

Chapter 3

"Mom, can Dad come over for dinner?"

Absolutely not! Jariah thought, opening the fridge and taking out the Tupperware container filled with last night's leftovers. The less time she spent with her ex the better, so inviting Wesley over to break bread after another stressful day of job interviews was definitely out of the question. "Not tonight, baby."

"But I haven't seen Daddy since my birthday party."

Hearing the anguish in her daughter's voice made her heart ache, but Jariah couldn't tell Ava the real reason her father wasn't coming around anymore. He was still trying to get back at her for breaking up with him, but the only person he was hurting was their daughter. "Your dad is busy at work, but he's always thinking about you, Ava, even when you're apart."

Ava sat at the kitchen table, playing with her stuffed animals, and when she poked out her bottom lip she looked just like her father. "I miss Daddy so much," she said. "He buys me ice cream and games and always tells me funny stories…"

Like most children, Ava adored her father and could go

on for hours about how wonderful he was. Jariah wasn't in the mood to talk about Wesley, but she let her baby girl talk, and resisted the urge to change the subject. Her ex was a decent father who spoiled their daughter silly, but he was a terrible boyfriend and a selfish lover. *Considering how inept he was in the bedroom, it's a miracle we ever got pregnant.*

Jariah's gaze drifted to the window above the sink. Birds chirped in the trees, girls played jump rope in the streets and the neighborhood watchdog, Mr. Regula, stood in his driveway, buffing his Cadillac to a shine. Aventura was a safe, caring community, filled with hardworking people, and Jariah enjoyed living in such a diverse, multicultural neighborhood.

"Mom, can we go to Chuck E. Cheese's tomorrow?" Ava asked, glancing up from her toys.

Jariah popped the leftovers in the microwave and set the timer for two minutes. "You have day camp tomorrow, remember?"

"I hate summer camp. It's boring and the kids are mean."

"Still not getting along with the other girls, huh?"

Her lips twisted into a scowl. "Laquinta called me a boo-boo head and pulled my braids."

"La who?"

When Ava giggled, her pigtails tumbled around her pretty, plump face.

"It doesn't matter what anyone says. You're beautiful."

"Just like you, right, Mama?"

"That's right, and don't you forget it." Jariah walked over to the table, cupped her daughter's chin and kissed the tip of her nose. "Put your toys away. It's time for dinner."

"Are we having pizza? I hope so. I just *love* cheese pizza."

"I'll make you pizza this weekend, but tonight we're having veggie casserole."

"Again? But we had that yesterday."

Overlooking her daughter's disappointment, Jariah opened the stove and heaved the casserole dish onto the counter.

"When I'm at Dad's house he lets me eat whatever I want," Ava announced. Marching over to the pantry, she tugged open the door and rummaged around inside. "I don't want leftovers. I want Froot Loops and chocolate chip cookies."

"Ava, cut it out. You're going to eat what I made for dinner and that's final."

"Why?" she demanded, her voice a shrill shout. "Why can't I eat what I want?"

"Because eating junk food will give you a tummy ache, and I don't want you to get sick."

"You always say no. You never give me what I want."

Feeling her temperature rise, Jariah cautioned herself to remain calm. Instead of scolding Ava for acting like a spoiled brat, she picked up the stuffed animals scattered on the table, and handed them to her daughter. "These need to go back to your room."

"I hate it here," Ava shouted. "I wish I lived with Daddy!"

Of course you do, Jariah thought sourly. *Your dad gives you whatever you want, and there are no rules at his house. It's one big party over there!* Releasing a deep sigh, she fought back the tears of frustration that threatened to break free. Ava's words hurt, made her question whether or not she was a good mother. Before self-pity could set in, Jariah shook off her thoughts and regarded her strong-willed daughter. "You can sit down at the table and eat dinner with me, or you can go to your room. It's your choice."

Ava stood there for a minute, her big, brown eyes narrowed as if weighing her options. Without a word, she took the toys out of Jariah's hands and moped down the hallway toward the stairwell. Her head was down, her shoulders were bent, and she moved like someone racked with grief.

Sadness flooded Jariah's heart. She felt a tightness in her chest that made it hard to breathe. It hurt to see her daughter like this, but what could she do? It wasn't her fault Ava hadn't seen her dad in a month, was it? These days, Wesley's visits were short and sporadic and more often than not he didn't show up at all. *Should I take him back? Should I move in with him for Ava's sake? Is that the answer to all of my problems?*

Chasing away the thought, Jariah returned to the stove and resumed preparing dinner. Taking Wesley back would be a mistake. He didn't love her—not the way she needed to be loved—and more importantly she didn't love him. Years ago, when they'd started dating at Miami University she'd naively thought Wesley was "the one." But after discovering she was pregnant, she'd seen a different side of him—a weak, spineless side that chose his parents repeatedly over her. And after years of playing second fiddle to his family, Jariah realized Wesley was never going to change, and broke things off for good. Contrary to what he thought, she deserved more, and didn't need him or anyone else to take care of her.

Hearing her cell phone ring, Jariah searched the kitchen for her BlackBerry. Spotting it on the breakfast bar, she scooped it up and read the number on the display. Luckily, it wasn't Wesley or his obnoxious mother. Jariah didn't recognize the number on the screen, but as she put her cell phone to her ear, she hoped and prayed it was someone calling to offer her a job. "Hello, Jariah Brooks speaking."

"Good evening, Jariah. This is Nicco Morretti. How are you?"

The sound of his deep, smooth voice tickled the tips of her ears.

"I'm great, thanks." Jariah knew why Nicco Morretti was calling, and for the first time since losing her job last month, she smiled from ear to ear. Excitement surged through her veins, hard and fast. Jariah wanted to dance around the kitchen, but she maintained her composure.

"I hope I haven't caught you at a bad time."

"No, not at all," she rushed to say. "I'm not doing anything. Now's a great time to talk."

"I'd like to discuss a business proposition with you."

Confused, Jariah scratched her head. A business proposition? Frowning, she stared down incredulously at the phone. *Did I get the account manager position or not?* she wondered, leaning against the granite countertop. "I'm sorry, Mr. Morretti, but I'm afraid I don't understand. What is this pertaining to?"

"I'd rather not discuss it over the phone."

Discuss what? I have no clue what you're talking about!

"Let's meet at Dolce Vita for drinks at eight o'clock."

"Tonight?"

"Yes, is that a problem?"

"Mom, look, I washed my hands with soap!" Ava stood beside the pantry door, waving her hands frantically in the air, hopping up and down as if she was on a pogo stick. "Can I have some cookies now?"

To quiet her daughter, Jariah pressed a finger to her lips, and steered her over to the table. "Is it okay if I call you back in an hour? I'm kind of in the middle of something."

"That's no problem at all," he said, his tone calm. "I'll talk to you then."

Jariah hung up and rested her phone on the kitchen counter. *What was* that *all about?* she wondered. *What is Nicco Morretti up to?* As Jariah fixed Ava a plate, she replayed her conversation with the cocky CEO in her head, trying to figure out if she'd missed something. But there was nothing to miss. Their conversation had been brief, and he'd been vague and mysterious throughout. The only way to find out what Nicco Morretti wanted was to meet him tonight at his restaurant, but first she had to find a babysitter.

Once Ava was eating dinner, Jariah slipped out of the kitchen and went into her bedroom. It was times like this that Jariah wished she could talk to her parents. She longed to hear her mother's voice and her father's booming laugh, but she knew they would never take her call. They had cut her out of their lives, and their bitter rejection still stung months later.

Ignoring the heaviness in her chest, Jariah flopped down on the bed, punched in her neighbor's phone number and waited anxiously for the call to connect. Cousins, Sadie and Felicia Robinson were good old-fashioned country girls, and Jariah loved hanging out with them. And so did her daughter. The cousins fussed over her, snuck her junk food when they thought Jariah wasn't looking, and gave Ava free reign of their town house.

"Hey, Sadie, how are you?" Jariah asked, greeting the thirty-five-year-old boutique owner with the fun-loving personality.

"I'm great. I was just about to make dinner. How is my sweet little honey pie doing?"

"Ava's fine, giving me sass and attitude as usual."

"Good for her!" Sadie cheered. "She needs to stand up for herself. You're way too strict."

"I have to be. Her dad is a total pushover," Jariah explained, feeling compelled to defend herself. "Ava throws a fit and he caves like a house of cards!"

The women laughed.

"Is Felicia still at work?" Jariah asked.

"No, she has a date."

"Another one? That's the third one this week and it's only Tuesday!"

"I know, tell me about it," Sadie quipped, her voice losing its cheer. "And the guy who picked her up tonight was a total hottie. Was driving a sports car and everything."

"You sound jealous."

"Why would I be jealous? I have a date, too."

"You do? With who?"

"The remote control!" Sadie giggled. "*Dating in the City* starts in fifteen minutes, and I can't wait to see what happens between Nelson Hamilton and the chick from…"

Jariah checked the time on the digital alarm clock, saw that it was almost six o'clock, and knew she had to rush things along. "Sadie, I need a favor," she began, clearing her throat. "Can you babysit Ava for me tonight? I know its short notice, but the CEO of Morretti Incorporated just called and asked me to meet him for drinks."

"No problem, girl. I'll be right over."

"There's no rush. I don't need to leave for another hour."

"I know," she said, "but I can smell your cooking all the way over here, and I'm hungrier than a plus-sized model on a no-carb diet!"

Jariah glanced at her wristwatch, and then tossed a look over her shoulder for the third time since arriving at Dolce Vita. When she'd entered the ritzy restaurant lounge and informed the hostess that she was meeting Nicco Morretti, the freckled brunette had greeted her warmly and escorted her to a secluded table in front of the picture window.

To pass the time, Jariah logged on to the internet and resumed reading an article she'd found that afternoon about Morretti Inc. Thanks to the magazine, she knew tons of information about the company and it's handsome CEO with the bold personality. Knowing the good, the bad and the ugly about Nicco Morretti made Jariah feel prepared and more confident about meeting him for drinks at his downtown restaurant.

A rich, heady aroma sweetened the air. A waitress sashayed through the lounge pushing a dessert cart, and Jariah hungrily licked her lips. A loud cheer went up from the table behind her, but she didn't pay the group any mind.

Dolce Vita was large, boisterous and busy, but the candle-lit tables, Italian marble and sable-brown decor created an intimate vibe. The restaurant lounge was the perfect setting for a romantic date, or a surprise marriage proposal, and as Jariah sat there, bored out of her mind, she reflected on the pitiful state of her love life. *Is Wesley right? Am I going to regret dumping him one day and beg him to take me back?*

Banishing the thought to the furthest corner of her mind, Jariah picked up her cocktail glass and slowly sipped through her straw. She longed to have someone special in her life, a man who would love her unconditionally. As she glanced around the room and saw all the starry-eyed couples toasting with wine flutes held high, she felt a stab of envy. *Am I ever going to meet Mr. Right? Or am I destined to spend my nights alone with no one to keep me company but my daughter and my girlfriends?*

Her thoughts turned to her parents, but instead of pushing her memories aside, she dialed their home number. As usual, the answering machine clicked on, and when it did, she took a deep breath and mustered all the cheer she had inside her. "Hi, Mom, and Dad, it's me, Jariah. I was just thinking about you, and wanted you to know that Ava and I miss you very much. We'd love to hear from you, so please give us a call. Bye."

Jariah pressed the end button on her phone and dropped it back into her purse.

"Can I interest you in another pineapple martini?"

"No, just the bill, thank you."

The waiter's eyes were wide with alarm, but he nodded and scurried off. He was back seconds later with the hostess in tow, fidgeting nervously with his hands.

"I just got off the phone with Mr. Morretti, and he asked me to apologize on his behalf," the hostess said, her tone contrite. "Can I get you another beverage while you wait?"

"No, thank you. I'd like the bill."

"The bill?" she repeated. "But Mr. Morretti is on his way."

"That's all fine and well, but he's already wasted enough of my time tonight." Jariah checked her watch, saw that it was eight-thirty, and stood to her feet. Cuddling in bed, reading with her daughter was the highlight of her day, and if she hurried she could still make it home in time to put Ava to bed. "The check, please."

"It's on the house."

"On the house?" Jariah frowned, confused by the hostess's words. "Why?"

"Because you're a personal guest of the owner."

Oh, of course. I bet all of his female guests eat for free.

"Thank you. Good night." Jariah tucked her black clutch bag under her arm. Walking through the lounge, she noted that every table was filled and that patrons were smiling, chatting and laughing. The waiting area was jam-packed, and as she strode past the aquarium, several men wearing wedding bands winked at her. Jariah rolled her eyes and kept on moving. Getting involved with a married man was asking for trouble, and Jariah avoided drama at all costs.

The evening air was thick and held the scent of rain. *Where had the summer gone?* Jariah wondered, striding through the restaurant parking lot. In a few short weeks, Ava would be back in school, and she'd be...

Jariah shuddered to think what she'd do if she still didn't have a job. Her car needed repairs, and Ava needed back-to-school clothes and supplies. If she didn't land an accounting position soon she'd have to stop doing all the things she loved—like taking Ava to the amusement park, sponsoring children in need and going for cocktails with her girlfriends.

"Jariah, wait up!"

Searching the parking lot for the face that matched that deep, husky voice, she slowed her pace and narrowed her eyes. And when her gaze landed on Nicco Morretti—looking all kinds of sexy in his fitted blue shirt and jeans, her feet froze to the ground.

Standing there with her heart pounding and her limbs shaking, Jariah decided that it should be a crime for a man to be *that* good-looking. A sin, actually, because all the thoughts that flooded her brain involved handcuffs, a blindfold and whip cream. The restaurateur oozed an intoxicating blend of masculinity and sensuality, and he moved like a tiger prowling the jungle.

"Good evening, Jariah. It's great to see you again."

Nicco stopped, just inches away from her face, and when Jariah got a whiff of his cologne her heart murmured inside her chest. The sexy CEO made her hyperventilate—his gaze was so powerful she felt vulnerable and exposed. Jariah hated the effect Nicco Morretti had on her, and wondered how she could be attracted to a guy who'd hit on anything with a pulse.

"I'm sorry I'm late." His voice was low, and he appeared apologetic. "Something important came up as I was leaving the office, and I couldn't get away."

Jariah didn't believe his story, not for a second, but she didn't question him. Why bother? He'd only lie, and besides, it didn't matter why he was late because she was leaving. Remembering their earlier conversation gave Jariah pause. She forced a sympathetic smile. "What did you want to discuss?"

"Not out here. Let's head back inside Dolce Vita."

"I was just leaving."

He cocked his head to the right. "I see that."

Jariah detected a hint of anger in his voice, and wondered what *that* was all about. *If anyone should be upset it should be me. You're thirty minutes late!* Confused by his reaction, she looked at him inquiringly.

"I invited you here so we could have a bite, and maybe get something—"

"I'm not hungry," she interrupted, annoyed by his blasé attitude. "I lost my appetite about *thirty* minutes ago."

"Then let me buy you a drink."

The feel of his hand along her bare shoulder weakened her resolve.

"I feel terrible for showing up late, but something came up that required my immediate attention," he explained. "I got here as soon as I could."

His explanation sounded plausible, reasonable even, but Jariah wasn't moved. Unsure of what to do, she vacillated between going home to her daughter and taking Nicco Morretti up on his offer. *This isn't a date,* she told herself, pushing her reservations to the back of her mind. *It's a business meeting and nothing more. I don't even like the guy.* But her tingling, inflamed body suggested otherwise. Her heartbeat roared in her ears, invisible beads of perspiration dotted her forehead and her sleeveless blouse stuck to her skin.

"Come back inside. I promise to make it worth your while."

To Jariah's utter disbelief and amazement, the word "yes" flew out of her mouth.

"Right this way." Nicco gestured to the restaurant with one hand and placed the other on the small of her back. "You look incredible tonight. Even more beautiful than I remember."

I do? The tips of her ears tingled, and her cheeks flushed with embarrassment. Commanding her legs to move and her hands to quit shaking, Jariah tried not to notice how dreamy Nicco Morretti looked or how delicious he smelled. Even though she was attracted to him, Jariah was determined not to be his next victim.

Tell that to your hot, lust-inflected body! her inner voice jeered. *You want Nicco Morretti so bad you can't even walk straight!*

Chapter 4

Nicco was having a hell of a time concentrating, and not just because Jariah Brooks was sitting across from him in his favorite corner booth at Dolce Vita looking like a million bucks. He found her worldly, sophisticated vibe appealing, and although the restaurant was loud and busy, he was having a kick-ass time in her company.

Boisterous conversation filled the restaurant, and all of the young, stylish diners were drinking, dancing and snapping pictures with their cell phones. From his seat, he had a bird's eye view of the lounge, and chuckled to himself when he spotted his head chef walking around greeting regulars, shaking hands and admonishing the tuxedo-clad waiters.

Like last night, the star power was definitely in abundance at Dolce Vita but to his surprise Jariah didn't get flustered or giddy when his celebrity friends dropped by their booth. She shook hands with each new arrival, but she seemed far more interested in her meal than chatting up A-list stars.

As Nicco surveyed the crowd, he wondered if he was being watched. Were the jerks who'd vandalized Dolce

Vita here tonight? Were they sitting at a table plotting their next move? Or at the bar keeping close tabs on him?

Anger burned inside him, and Nicco gripped his tumbler so hard he feared the glass would shatter into a hundred pieces. The police had given up searching for suspects, so it was up to him to find out who had trashed his restaurant. And he would. No matter the cost.

At the bar, Nicco spotted a slim, bald-headed man wearing dark sunglasses in deep conversation with one of the female bartenders, and he sat up taller, straighter. The stranger resembled his ex-friend and former business partner, Tye Caldwell. Nicco considered going into the lounge to find out for sure, but decided against it. Tye wouldn't be stupid enough to show his face at Dolce Vita after what happened last summer, would he? Nicco squinted, and peered inconspicuously around the young Asian couple sharing a steamy French kiss. The lights were low, and the lounge was packed, which made it impossible for him to get a good look at the well-dressed man. Thinking about, Tye—someone he'd once considered family—filled his heart with pain. Nicco felt a twinge of deep sadness. *First Tye screws me over, and then Gracie. Are there any honest, trustworthy people left in the world?* he wondered. *If my closest friend and confidant could betray me, then anyone can.*

"I'm glad I let you talk me into ordering the *vitello*. It's so moist and creamy…"

Nicco ditched his thoughts and turned his attention to his lovely dinner companion with the knock-out curves. He was a leg man, but couldn't resist admiring Jariah's other impressive physical assets. The twenty-seven-year-old beauty was glowing, radiating an inner light that literally lit up the whole restaurant. She smelled like cherry blossoms, spoke with confidence, and despite her youth, carried herself in a composed, mature way. Her ruffled, orange blouse was eye-catching and showed off her toned arms and a hint of cleavage.

"I'm glad that you're enjoying your meal," Nicco said, eying her over the rim of his glass. "If you'd like, I could order you another entrée."

"No, thank you. I've had more than enough food for one evening."

"Does that mean you're not having dessert?"

"I can't. I'm teaching a step-aerobics class in the morning, and if I pig out tonight I won't be able to keep up with my students."

Her beauty dazzled him, made him forget everyone else in the room. Nicco didn't know if it was the wine or the lively atmosphere in the lounge that helped loosen her up, but it was obvious Jariah was in great spirits. While waiting for their entrees to arrive, she'd asked smart, insightful questions about his company, and impressed him with her vast knowledge of the stock market. Jariah spoke with enthusiasm and passion about her volunteering work, and chatted excitedly about the new projects she'd developed at the Miami Food Bank.

"I'd love to discuss your business proposition now," Jariah said, setting aside her plate.

Clasping her hands together, she looked him straight in the eye, her gaze unwavering and intense. It held him in its powerful grip, refused to let him go, and for the second time that night Nicco hoped he didn't look as stupid as he felt. "I'd rather hear more about your hobbies and interests," he said, artfully dodging the question. "What do you do when you're not teaching fitness classes at Premier Fitness?"

"Not much. Now, back to your business proposition—"

"Come l'aragosta era? Fido di che sia stato anche il suo amare, Sig. Morretti."

Chef Gambro, an overweight man of fifty, bounded over

to the booth and clapped Nicco vigorously on the back. Speaking in Italian, his voice stern, but his manner playful, he explained that he was on a date and didn't want to be interrupted. Nicco saw Jariah tense, then raise a perfectly arched eyebrow, and wondered if she'd understood what he'd said.

Gambro turned to Jariah and took her hand. Lifting it to his mouth, he reverently kissed her palm. Gazing at her adoringly, he complimented her effusively in his native tongue, but before Nicco could answer on Jariah's behalf she responded—in Italian. Her tone was refreshingly light, but she spoke in a voice as lively and as animated as Chef Gambro's. Dumbfounded, Nicco leaned forward in his seat, unable to believe his ears.

"Grazie per un pasto meraviglioso, Chef Gambro voi. Tutto era spettacolare, e il vitello era il migliore che abbia mai avuto..."

Nicco listened, enraptured, and realized that Jariah Brooks was as gracious as she was kind. She thanked Chef Gambro for a delicious meal and promised to return soon for more of his spectacular Italian cooking. The chef beamed, and when he swaggered back to the kitchen seconds later, his chest puffed up with pride.

"You speak Italian?" Nicco asked, regaining the use of his tongue.

"Yes, and Spanish, as well."

"That's impressive."

"I had no choice. My parents forced me to take foreign language classes for years."

"That must have been a total drag."

"It was. My parents had very high expectations for me, and..." Jariah winced, as if she had a toothache, and her expression turned somber. "I owe all of my success to them."

Silence settled at the table like an unwelcomed guest.

"Tell me more about you background, Jariah."

The corners of her mouth tightened. "What do you want to know that we haven't already discussed tonight?"

Everything! he thought, draping an arm over the back of the booth. *Do you feel the chemistry between us? Have you ever had a summer fling? Would you like to?*

To keep from reaching across the table, and caressing her skin, Nicco picked up his glass tumbler and downed the rest of his cognac. He started to ask Jariah about her career aspirations, but she interrupted him and repeated the same question she'd posed earlier—the one he'd conveniently forgot. Nicco was enjoying their conversation, and wasn't ready to discuss his business proposition just yet. He wanted to hear more about her family, what she liked doing in her free time, and the kind of guys she dated. Not because he was interested in her, but because he planned to hire her, and felt it was important to know as much about her as possible, he had convinced himself.

"Did I get the account manager position?"

Nicco heard the vulnerability in her voice, saw the twinkle in her eyes and felt the impulse to lie. But he knew there'd be hell to pay if he upset Mrs. Reddick, and the HR Director was dead-set against hiring Jariah. Besides, he had something better in mind for her, and couldn't wait to see the look on her face when he shared the good news. "No, Jariah, I'm sorry, you didn't."

Her smile faded. "Why not? My interview went so well."

"You're right, it did," he conceded, troubled by the pained expression on her face. "But we decided to hire someone with more experience."

Jariah swallowed hard. "I understand."

Driven by compassion, Nicco reached across the table and touched her hand. Jariah jerked away, as if he'd zapped her with a stun gun, and pressed herself flat against the booth.

"You invited me down here to tell me I didn't get the job?"

He heard the accusation in her voice and rushed to explain. "No, of course not. I need an executive assistant, and thought you might be interested in the position."

Her eyes tapered, and a scowl stained her lush, red lips. "I'm not."

"Don't you want to hear the job description before you turn it down?"

"No, Mr. Morretti, I don't."

"Please, call me, Nicco."

"No offense, *Mr. Morretti,* but I have no desire to be a glorified receptionist."

He paused to organize his thoughts. Jariah's reaction was unsettling, and he didn't understand why she was glaring at him. "I don't need a receptionist. I already have one," he explained. "I need someone to manage my schedule, accompany me to various meetings, liaise with clients and respond to my correspondence in a timely and professional manner."

"Thanks, but no thanks."

"Let me finish, there's more," he said calmly, though his temperature raised a notch. "My older brother and I oversee the day-to-day operations of Morretti Incorporated, but my real passion is the restaurant business. I love acquiring struggling establishments and turning them around, and I need someone with passion and conviction to help me."

The waiter arrived, refilled their wineglasses and cleared the table of their dinner plates. He departed seconds later, but Nicco didn't speak. He thought of telling a joke to lighten the mood, but decided against it when he saw her sneak a glance at her silver watch. Jariah looked bored, wouldn't meet his gaze, and the tension hovering above their table was suffocating.

"I travel considerably for business, and have trips to

Los Angeles, Chicago and Washington planned this year. Also," he paused, to allow sufficient time for his words to sink in, "Morretti Inc. has numerous opportunities for employee advancement, and the next time there's a vacancy in the accounting department I would personally recommend you."

"Sorry, but I'm still not interested." Jariah stood, purse in hand, and eyed him coolly. "Thanks for dinner. Good night."

Determined to prolong their time together, Nicco slid out of the booth and boldly stepped in front of her, getting so close he could smell her strawberry-flavored lip gloss. "Let's discuss the position further over a round of drinks," he proposed, gesturing across the room. Every stool at the bar was taken, but he'd find a seat for her. Hell, he'd clear the entire bar if he had to. It was obvious Jariah was disappointed and upset, but Nicco didn't understand why. She should be jumping up and down for joy, not tapping her foot impatiently on the ground and shooting evil daggers at him. "Hear me out. You won't be sorry."

"I can't support my daughter on minimum wage."

Nicco gave her arm a light squeeze. Her skin was soft, and her spicy, floral perfume aroused his senses. And his erection. "I'd never pay someone with your qualifications seven dollars an hour," he said honestly. "Your salary would be sixty-thousand dollars, plus benefits, and three weeks paid vacation."

Nicco studied her reaction, and tried to surmise what she was thinking. Her face was blank, impossible to read, but he knew she was impressed. Had to be. He was offering her a great job package, and the opportunity to work at a successful, world-renowned company. "Take some time to think it over."

"There's nothing to think about."

"I think there is. I spoke to your references this morning, and—"

Her eyes doubled in size. "You did?"

"Yes, and your old boss at First National Trust Bank gave you a glowing recommendation," he said, nodding his head. "He said you were the best accountant he'd ever had, and one of the smartest, too. And now that I know you speak Italian, I'm even more convinced that you're the right person for the executive assistant position."

Too choked up to speak, Jariah stared down at the floor, wishing it would open up and swallow her into the ground. The weight of her disappointment was crushing, so heavy she couldn't look Nicco in the eye. Convinced she'd landed the account manager's job, she'd imagined herself signing the contracts at Dolce Vita, and toasting her success over a glass of rose champagne. But it wasn't to be.

Could this evening get any worse? What's he going to do next? Ask me to do his laundry? Jariah shook off her thoughts and her feelings of utter despair. This wouldn't be the first time a man had ruined her night, and it probably wouldn't be the last time. Agreeing to meet Nicco was a mistake, and as Jariah blinked back the tears that formed in her eyes, she regretted ever coming to the restaurant to meet with him.

"Are you sure you can't join me at the bar for a glass of merlot?"

Scared her emotions would break free if she spoke, Jariah shook her head and opened her purse in search of her keys.

"I'll walk you to your car."

"No, thank you. I can manage."

Nicco leaned in close and grazed his fingers across her bare shoulder. A thousand volts of electricity rushed through her body. For a moment, Jariah lost herself in the depths of his deep brown eyes. She feared he was going to kiss her right then and there in the middle of the dining room, and didn't know whether to run or hide.

Clapping and spirited singing rang out behind her, and just like that, their spell was broken. Turning on her heels, Jariah blew out of the dining room at lightning-fast speed. Anxious to put as much distance as possible between herself and Nicco Morretti, she marched briskly through the restaurant, and out the front doors into the starry, summer night.

Minutes later, Jariah was sitting inside of her Dodge Plymouth with her face buried in her hands. Her thoughts were on dinner and the time she'd spent getting to know Nicco Morretti. From the moment they'd been seated in the restaurant, he'd been warm and complimentary, and even agreed that she'd nailed her job interview on Monday. But instead of offering her the account manager position, he'd insulted her.

"What a jerk," Jariah grumbled, putting on her seat belt. "He must do recreational drugs because his business proposition is the most ludicrous thing I've ever heard!"

Jariah jammed the key in the ignition and turned the lock. The engine coughed and sputtered but didn't start. "Oh, no, not again." Taking a deep breath, she closed her eyes and counted to ten. Feeling calmer, she tried the key again. And again. On the third try, the engine roared to life, and Jariah sighed in relief.

As she drove out of the restaurant parking lot, she spotted Nicco Morretti standing in front of Dolce Vita, lighting a cigar. Smoke billowed around him, adding to his mysterious, bad-boy allure. Pretending she didn't see him, she returned her attention to the road and stepped on the gas pedal. His words played in her mind, wounding her afresh.

You showed a lot of poise and professionalism during your interview, but we decided to hire someone with more experience in the accounting field.

Tears spilled down her cheeks, but Jariah furiously slapped them away. She didn't have time to cry; she had a daughter to take care of and a full-time job to find. Jariah told herself that she was stressing over nothing, that she'd be gainfully employed in no time, but her doubts and frustrations remained.

Sweat drenched her skin, and the fear of losing everything she held dear—her independence, her home and custody of her daughter—burned inside the walls of her chest. *What am I doing wrong?* Jariah wondered, drumming her fingers on the steering wheel. *How many more interviews do I have to go on before someone hires me?* Jariah didn't know what she was going to do when the money in her emergency fund ran out, but there was one thing she knew for sure: the next time she saw Nicco Morretti she was running the other way.

Chapter 5

Laughter, pop music and the heady scent of fresh straw-berries drifted out the kitchen window in Jariah's town-home. Despite the cheerful atmosphere inside and the mouth-watering aromas sweetening the night air, she dragged herself up the stone walkway. Not because she was tired, but because she didn't want to answer Sadie's incessant questions about her business meeting with Nicco Morretti.

At the front door, Jariah shook off her melancholy mood and fussed with her hair. She didn't want Sadie to know that she'd been crying, so as she unlocked the door she arched her bent shoulders and plastered a smile on her face.

Inside the kitchen, fixing themselves a snack were Sadie and Jariah's cousin, Felicia. The thirty-year-old divorcee had a flamboyant personality, and was such a social butter-fly, she had no trouble making friends. Or meeting hand-some, successful men, either. Her silky hair was touched with honey-blonde streaks, and her zebra-print body suit was so tight, Jariah wondered if she could breathe.

"Hey, you guys, what's up?" Jariah dumped her things on the end table and joined her friends at the breakfast bar. It was covered with junk food, movies and fashion magazines.

"We're just making a late-night snack." Felicia opened the tub of ice-cream and dunked her spoon inside. "Do you want a chocolate sundae with caramel syrup?"

"No thanks. I just ate." Jariah sat down on a stool and plucked a strawberry out of the fruit bowl. The oversized glass dish was a gift from her mom for her birthday. Every time she looked at it her heart ached. "Felicia, I'm surprised you're here. I thought you had a date."

"I did, but the guy turned out to be a dud, so I faked a migraine and came home."

"Wow, that's harsh."

"Not to me," she chirped. "If the chemistry isn't there, I leave. No exceptions."

Sadie piped up. "I agree. I don't have time to waste with Mr. Wrong or Mr. Maybe. My biological clock is ticking so loud my mother can hear it all the way in Tennessee!"

The cousins hooted and laughed.

"How was Ava?" Jariah glanced up at the staircase to the second floor, where Ava's bedroom was, and imagined her adorable daughter curled up in her Dora the Explorer bed sleeping soundly. "I hope she didn't give you any trouble."

"Not at all. She fell asleep twenty minutes after you left." Sadie ripped open a bag of Doritos chips and popped one into her mouth. "Since Ava was already in her pj's, I carried her to her room and tucked her in."

"Thank you, girl. You always take such great care of my baby."

"It's my pleasure. I love Ava. She's smart and saucy just like me!" When Sadie laughed, her short, thick curls tumbled around her pretty oval face. "How did things go tonight?"

"Yes, do tell." Felicia faked a swoon. "I love Italian

men, and when Sadie told me you had a date with Nicco Morretti, I almost creamed my panties!"

"It wasn't a date. He wanted to discuss a business proposition with me."

"Did you get the account manager job?" Sadie asked.

"No. They gave it to someone with more experience."

Felicia put her bowl down on the breakfast bar. "I don't understand. The guy invited you to his restaurant just to tell you that you didn't get the job? Wow, that's cold!"

"He wants me to be his assistant," Jariah explained, still unable to believe it herself.

"I bet that's not all he wants," Felicia drawled, eyebrows raised.

"Ignore her, girl. Congratulations. When do you start?"

"I don't. I told him thanks, but no thanks."

Sadie wore a confused face. "Why? Working for Nicco Morretti would be a huge coup."

"I didn't bust my butt in college just to end up being a glorified secretary."

"What's wrong with being a secretary?" Felicia asked, cocking an eyebrow.

"Nothing, but it's not the right career for me."

"Why not?"

"Because I went to school for accounting, not to fetch coffee and answer phones."

"I was a receptionist back in Chattanooga," Felicia said, pointing at her chest. "I made decent money, and I was employee of the month twice."

"I wasn't trying to imply that I'm better than you—"

Felicia sucked her teeth. "Sure you weren't."

Jariah felt trapped, like a rabbit cornered by a coyote in the woods. She feared if she didn't apologize to Felicia, their relationship would be irretrievably damaged, but before she could even think about what to say, Sadie spoke up.

"Tell us more about the executive assistant position." Leaning forward on her stool, her expression curious, she propped a hand under her chin and waited expectantly. "What's the job description? Is there a signing bonus? Do you have to work evenings and weekends?"

Reluctantly, Jariah recounted her conversation with Nicco Morretti. The night was a blur, clouded by intense gazes, blinding chemistry and disappointments. The only thing she remembered clearly was the moment Nicco had touched her. His hands were warm, strong and they set her body ablaze. "After he told me I didn't get the account manager position, I kinda zoned out, so I don't remember the specifics of the EA position besides the sixty-thousand-dollar salary."

"Sixty-thousand dollars is great money."

"Amen to that," Felicia quipped. "Shoot, if you won't take the job, I will!"

"I'm surprised you didn't jump at the offer, especially in light of the rent increase."

Jariah frowned and shot Sadie a questioning look. "What are you talking about?"

"Didn't you get a letter from the condominium board yesterday?"

"No, why? What did it say?"

"On September 1st, our rent and condo fees are increasing by eight percent."

Felicia threw her hands up in the air. "Oh, great, there goes my mani-pedi money."

It's been so long, I can't even remember the last time I went to the salon, Jariah thought sadly. *I wish I could get my hair done, and update my wardrobe, too, but I just can't afford it.*

Her gaze fell across the calendar and zeroed in on the date. Jariah had a full day ahead of her tomorrow, but she wasn't excited about any of her upcoming interviews. Job hunting was stressful, but throwing in the towel wasn't an option. She was going to find a full-time job—no if, ands or buts about it. And when she did she was buying herself a new car, because she was sick of hearing her Dodge cough and sputter.

"I think you should take the EA job. It's the smart thing to do," Sadie said emphatically. "Take the position, and if something better comes along, just quit."

"Mr. Morretti's going to want me to sign a one-year contract."

"So what? People break contracts every day." Felicia flipped her hair over her shoulders, and gave a nonchalant shrug. "It's no big deal. What's he going to do? Sue you?"

Jariah gave serious consideration to what her girlfriends said, but still wasn't convinced. "I don't think I can…" She broke off speaking, and shook her head. "Forget it."

"What is it?" Sadie asked, resting a hand on her shoulder. "What's bothering you?"

"I'm scared of what people will say when they find out I'm a receptionist."

And by people, I mean my parents. I've disappointed them so many times, and I don't want them to hear how much of a failure I am. Jariah stared at the framed photograph on the wall. It had been taken the day of her high school graduation, long before college, wild frat parties, and Wesley Covington came along. Back then, her parents had had complete control of her life, and Jariah had been so anxious to break free she'd applied to dozens of out-of-state universities. The day she'd received her acceptance letter to Miami University she'd danced around the kitchen, feeling like the luckiest girl alive. To this day, it still amazed her how young and naive she'd been. If she hadn't been so trusting, and head over heels in love with Wesley—the first guy she'd ever kissed—she never would have gotten pregnant her senior year.

The thought froze in Jariah's brain. Scared of where her emotions would take her, she shook her head to ward off the memories that threatened to break free. Thinking about the day she broke the news of her pregnancy to her parents always brought feelings of guilt, shame and regret. Jariah had enough on her plate to deal with without adding the mistakes of her past to the mix. Her rent was going up, she had no job prospects, and her car was on its last leg. *What more could possibly go wrong this week? Am I ever going to catch a break?*

"Who cares what people say?" Sadie gave Jariah a one-armed hug. "You'll be making an honest living, and that's all that matters."

"I couldn't agree more." Felicia peeked inside Jariah's purse, took out her cell phone and offered it to her. "Go on. Call him."

"Who?" Jariah asked, playing dumb.

"That Italian heartthrob with the bedroom eyes, of course!"

"I need to sleep on it."

"Tomorrow might be too late," Felicia said, her tone grave.

Jariah folded her arms. "Why are you pressuring me? What's in this for you?"

"I'm just being a good friend."

"Right, and you're a natural blonde!" Sadie quipped, her tone full of attitude and sarcasm. "You're up to something. I just know it."

Felicia batted her fake eyelashes. "Who, me?"

"Yes, you. Come clean. Why do you want Jariah to work for Morretti Inc. so bad?"

"Because Nicco's older brother, Rafael, is exactly my type!"

Giggling, the cousins exchanged high-fives.

"How do you know so much about the Morretti family?" Jariah asked.

Felicia waved her BlackBerry in the air. "Google, of course!"

"I almost forgot. I got our tickets to the Kings of R & B concert this morning." Sadie unzipped her handbag, took out her wallet and handed a ticket to Jariah. "Don't worry about paying me back until you get a job. I know you're good for it."

"This ticket's a hundred and fifty bucks!" she complained. "I can't afford that."

"You could if you took the executive assistant job," Felicia pointed out.

"It's not about the position or even the pay," Jariah confessed. "Nicco Morretti thinks he's God's gift to women and I honestly couldn't imagine working for him."

"No one says you have to love the guy. Just do your job and collect your paycheck!"

"It's a good thing you have Wesley's child support payments to help keep you afloat—"

Jariah cut Sadie off, annoyed at what she was implying. "I can't use Ava's money to pay my living expenses. That wouldn't be right."

The women exchanged curious glances.

"But you've been out of work for months," Felicia said. "How are you getting by?"

"I'm using my emergency fund, and when that runs out I'll just sell my car."

"Girl, please, you couldn't *give* that old hoopty away, let alone sell it!"

The women cracked up.

"I'm going to go check on, Ava." Jariah finished her orange juice and stood. "Thanks again for watching her you guys. I really appreciate it."

Sadie picked up one of the DVDs on the counter and

held it up in the air. "We were about to watch *Think Like A Man,* but if you're turning in we'll skedaddle."

For effect, Jariah licked her lips and fanned a hand to her face. "And miss my chance to see my future husband, Michael Ealy, on the big screen? No way! I'll be right back."

Jariah climbed the staircase, thinking about the advice her girlfriends had given her. An hour ago, she'd stormed out of Dolce Vita, vowing never to speak to Nicco Morretti again, but now she wondered if she'd acted in haste.

Dismissing the thought, she decided rejecting the CEO's business proposition was the right thing to do. *I'll have a new job by the end of the week,* Jariah pledged, more determined than ever to find a position in her field. *And it damn sure won't be a lowly receptionist position.*

Chapter 6

The first thing Jariah did when she returned home from picking up Ava from day camp on Thursday afternoon was check her answering machine for missed calls. It had been a week since her last interview, and Jariah was running out of options *and* money. There were no new messages, no lucrative job offers, and as she sank into her favorite chair in the bright and airy living room, she became overcome with feelings of hopelessness. Her body felt weighed down with stress and fatigue—Jariah knew it would be a struggle to stand up.

"Mom, can I play outside?"

Her vision was blurred by the unshed tears in her eyes, but Jariah nodded and said, "Sure, sweetie, but stay in front of the house. No wandering off, okay?"

"Okay, Mom. I won't."

Jariah heard the front door open and close. Shrieks of laughter gushed through the window, and the hot, blustery wind ruffled the curtains.

Thinking about her situation caused a tear to skid down her cheek. Being at home, day-in and day-out, while her friends were at their respective jobs was discouraging, but Jariah wasn't sure of what else she could do to fix her situation.

To take her mind off her troubles, she turned to the stack of mail she'd dumped on the side table. Scooping it up, she dumped the letters in her lap and propped her legs up on the coffee table. As Jariah scanned the electricity bill, she realized that she'd been a fool to turn down Nicco Morretti's business proposition. Despite applying to dozens of companies, the executive assistant position was all she had, her one and only offer. And now that Jariah had realized the error of her ways she wasn't going to let the opportunity slip through her grasp.

Sitting up, Jariah took her cell phone out of her purse, found Nicco Morretti's number in the call history, and after hitting Send, she waited for him to pick up. Her heart threatened to explode from her chest, but she carefully rehearsed what she wanted to say.

"Daddy!"

Frowning, Jariah stood and strode over to the window. She pulled back the curtains just in time to see Ava race down the walkway and leap into Wesley's open arms. Jariah was annoyed that her ex had showed up unannounced, but she decided not to give him a hard time. He'd come to spend time with his daughter, and seeing them together warmed her heart. Ava was beaming, fiercely clutching her dad's hand, and proudly showing him off to the neighborhood kids, as if he was a new toy.

The phone beeped in her ear, cuing her to leave a message, but Jariah hung up. She'd call Nicco later, once Wesley was gone. Deciding to get started on dinner, she went into the kitchen and put her cell phone down on the counter. Jariah opened the fridge and took out everything she needed to make chili. Within seconds, the vegetables were chopped and the stew was bubbling.

Just because I don't have a job doesn't mean I should

mope around feeling sorry for myself, Jariah decided, mincing a clove of garlic. *Especially when Wesley's around. The last thing I need is him getting on my case.* Back when they were living together, he constantly teased her about being a stay-at-home mom, and joked that she sat around all day watching TV and eating bon-bons while he slaved away at work. That irritated Jariah, but not as much as his disrespect and total disregard for her feelings.

The front door slammed shut, and footsteps pounded on the hardwood floor.

"Good afternoon, Jariah. How have you been?"

"I'm fine thanks, and you?"

"Great, now that I'm with my number one girl." Wesley scooped Ava up in his arms and spun her around in the air. "I finished work early, so I decided to stop by. If you girls aren't busy, I'd love to take you out for dinner. How about we go to our favorite spot?"

"Ava, Daddy's going to take you to Groovy's Pizza. Isn't that wonderful?"

"Yahoo! Let's go!"

"Why don't you go change into one of the pretty new party dresses Grandma Stella bought you for your birthday?" Jariah suggested, cupping her daughter's shoulder and steering her out of the kitchen. "And don't forget to wash up."

"Stay right there, Dad. I'll be right back."

Jariah waited until Ava raced out of the kitchen before she spoke to Wesley.

"Next time you're in the mood to drop by, please call first."

"I'll keep that in mind." He looked her up and down. "I see that you've stopped going to the gym."

"I'm a certified fitness instructor, thank you very much."

His eyebrows drew together and formed a long, crooked

line. "I find that hard to believe. You've definitely put on weight since the last time I saw you."

And you're a lousy lover, but you don't see me warning the female masses via Twitter, do you? "It's a lovely day," she said, gesturing to the door he'd just arrogantly swaggered through. "Why don't you wait for Ava outside?"

He chuckled, as if she'd just told him a knock-knock joke, then leaned casually against the breakfast bar. "Have you found a new job?"

"No, but I've had several promising offers this week."

And by several, I mean one, but whose counting?

"I'm happy for you," he said tightly, his jaw clenched. "We'll celebrate at dinner."

Jariah held her tongue. She hated when Wesley showed up unannounced and expected her to drop everything. But instead of cursing him out in every language she knew, she picked up the wooden spoon and stirred the pot of chili. "I'm not going with you guys. I have housework to do." It was a lie, and Jariah knew Wesley wouldn't believe her, but she didn't care what her ex thought. They weren't a couple anymore, and if not for Ava, she'd have nothing to do with him or his bougie parents.

"Is something wrong with your cell?" Wesley swiped her BlackBerry off the counter and examined it. "My mom said every time she calls you your phone goes straight to voice mail."

Raising an eyebrow as if confused, Jariah said, "Is Stella calling about something specific, or to cram her new-age parenting philosophies down my throat?"

"She wants to take Ava to Orlando in August. Is that cool with you?"

"I'll check my schedule and get back to you."

"I have your child support check for this month." Wearing a broad grin, Wesley reached into his back pocket, took out an envelope and offered it to her. "Don't blow it all at Macy's."

Jariah dropped the spoon on the counter. "I've never, *ever,* used Ava's money on myself. I pay for her extracurricular activities, and put the rest away in her savings account."

"Sure you do." Wesley dropped the envelope on the breakfast bar. "You've been out of work for months, and I know your parents aren't helping you, so you must be using Ava's child support checks to help stay afloat."

"I'm telling you the truth," she argued, struggling to control her temper. "I have no reason to lie, *and* I have the bank account statements to prove it."

"You know," he began, lowering his voice a notch, "I'm not dating anyone."

Jariah rolled her eyes. "Good for you."

"I want you and Ava to come back home. We're a family, and we should be together."

"I want to be a wife, and I'd love to have two or three more children. Don't you?"

Wesley coughed and raked a hand over his short, brown hair. He looked uncomfortable, and was restlessly shuffling his feet.

"That's what I thought."

"Jariah, we've been over this a million times. I'm just not ready," he said sternly, as if he was admonishing an errant child. "We'll get married one day. I promise."

"One day isn't good enough, Wesley. We've been arguing back and forth about this for years, and I'm tired of it."

"You've been tripping ever since you started reading Dr. Rashondra Brown's stupid self-help books," he argued, scowling. "You should be thanking your lucky stars that I'm a good man because I know a lot of single moms who don't have it as good as you."

Jariah propped a hand on her hip. "Is that so?"

"It sure is. Their exes are all trifling, dead-beat dads who don't give them diddly squat."

"And you should be thanking your lucky stars that I was a patient, understanding girlfriend because I don't know anyone who'd put up with you *or* your mother for five years."

"You're never going to find anyone better than me."

"Why?" she replied, snorting a laugh. "Because you're *such* a great catch?"

"No, because I can afford to buy you anything you want. Clothes, jewelry, purses—"

"I want a commitment, Wesley, not another Hermès bag."

Muttering in response, he thrust his hands into the pockets of his dark, tailored slacks. His gaze bounced around the room, looking everywhere but at her face.

"I'm ready." Entering the kitchen, Ava curtseyed, and then did a twirl around the breakfast bar. "Daddy, do you like my dress?"

Wesley's smile returned. "I love it, sweetheart. You look like a princess."

"Be a good girl," Jariah admonished, adjusting the straps on Ava's pink floral sundress. "Have fun with Daddy, and don't give him any trouble."

"I won't, Mom. I'll be on my best behavior."

Jariah kissed Ava on the cheek and gave her a hug. "See you later, alligator."

"In a while, crocodile!"

She stood in the doorway, waving at Ava, but the second Wesley's Range Rover turned out of the condominium complex, she snatched up her cell phone and hit Redial. Time was of the essence, and Jariah feared if she waited until tomorrow to contact Nicco, it would be too late. She needed that executive assistant position now, and was willing to humble herself to get it. Jariah hated the thought of doing the CEO's bidding, but she'd rather work at Morretti Inc. than spend another day at home waiting for the telephone to ring.

"This is Nicco Morretti."

His voice filled the line, warming her all over. Her heart rate spiked, but Jariah cautioned herself to remain focused. She was attracted to Nicco, but he wasn't her type, definitely not the kind of guy she'd ever fall for, and flirting with him would only bring trouble. "Yes, hello, this is… ah…ah…" Jariah drew a blank, and wanted to slap herself for forgetting her own name.

"It's great to hear from you, Jariah. I hope you and your daughter are doing well."

Staring down at the phone, her mouth agape, Jariah was convinced she'd misheard him. *He recognizes my voice? But we've only spoken on the phone once!*

"I, um, feel terrible about the way I acted last week at Dolce Vita, and I want to apologize." Jariah cringed at the memory of that night, but pushed past her shame and spoke from the heart. "I was disappointed because I didn't get the account manager job, and I let my emotions get the best of me. I'm sorry."

"I understand, Jariah. It happens to the best of us," he said sympathetically. "Even me."

"Really?"

"Absolutely."

He chuckled, and the knot in her chest loosened, abated.

"Remind me to tell you about the time I lost my cool and slugged a retired navy SEAL."

"No way. You didn't."

"I did, and I have his medical bills to prove it!"

Jariah laughed. She didn't know if Nicco was serious or just tying to make her feel better, but to her surprise, he did.

"I hope you're calling about the executive assistant position, because I could really use someone with your skill and expertise in my office."

Jariah swallowed a laugh. Making coffee didn't require any skill or expertise, but she was smart enough not to argue with him. "The position is still available?"

"It's yours if you want it."

"That's great. Thanks so much. When would you like me to start?"

"How does tomorrow sound?"

"But tomorrow is Friday."

"I know. Is that a problem?"

"No, not at all," Jariah rushed to say, again feeling foolish for letting her nerves get the best of her. "What time would you like me to be at the office?"

"Nine o'clock sharp."

"Nine o'clock it is."

"I'm excited about you joining the Morretti Inc. family," he said after a beat. "I think we're going to make a dynamic team."

"I agree, and I'm really looking forward to seeing you tomorrow morning." Stunned by her loose, wayward tongue, Jariah cupped a hand over her mouth. *I can't believe I just said that! What was I thinking?*

"Get a good night's sleep, Jariah." His tone was filled with an intoxicating blend of heat and sensuality. "Tomorrow's going to be an exciting day. One you won't ever forget."

Chapter 7

Morretti Incorporated was housed inside a ten-story building located in the heart of downtown Miami on a street lined with billboards, palm trees and colorful flowers. It was surrounded by soaring skyscrapers, trendy art galleries and high-end restaurants and cafés frequented by local celebrities and gossip-hungry socialites.

Locking her car doors, Jariah swung her purse over her shoulder and strode briskly across the parking lot. Her palms were drenched with sweat, and her legs were wobbling, but she managed to march confidently through the sliding glass doors and identify herself to the impeccably dressed redhead manning the front desk.

In the reception area, Jariah drank a cup of coffee and read the *Miami Herald*—twice. Thirty minutes passed, but she remained upbeat, happy to be at Morretti Incorporated, instead of at home perusing the classifieds. But after an hour of waiting for her new boss and watching other employees come and go, Jariah's good mood fizzled. *Is he ever on time?* she wondered, peering outside the front window in search of him. *Doesn't he know how rude it is to keep people waiting? Does he even care?*

"Ms. Brooks, good morning."

Jariah spotted the HR director traipsing across the lobby and stood. "Good morning, Mrs. Reddick," she said brightly. "How are you?"

"I understand that you're coming on board."

"Yes, I am, and I'm very excited to be here. I look forward to working with you and the rest of the Morretti Incorporated team."

"I must confess, Ms. Brooks, I was quite surprised when Mr. Morretti told me the news." A sneer curled her peach lips. "Don't you think being an assistant is beneath you?"

Jariah choked on her tongue. Taken aback by the question and Ms. Reddick's curt tone, she schooled her features to remain impassive, unperturbed. She didn't know if it was a rhetorical question, and didn't know how to respond. What was she supposed to say? *I don't want to be an executive assistant, and I think Nicco is going to be a handful, but I've been out of work for months, and I have no other job prospects. But don't worry, Mrs. Reddick, as soon as I find an accountant manager position, I'm out of here!*

"I need to review the orientation packet with you, so be at my office at one o'clock."

"That sounds great. I really appreciate you making the time to meet with me."

"Don't forget to bring a voided check and two pieces of ID for your personnel file."

Jariah nodded her head in understanding.

"Very well. I will see you this afternoon."

"Is there anything you need me to do?"

Lines of confusion wrinkled Mrs. Reddick's face. "Excuse me?"

"Nicco isn't…" Jariah saw the HR director's eyebrows shoot up, and broke off speaking. Adopting a professional tone, she said, "Mr. Morretti isn't here yet, so I was hoping I could help out in your department until he arrives."

"No, thank you. I'm busy training new employees, and you'd just be in the way."

"Can you point me in the direction of the accounting department then?" Jariah was disappointed that Mrs. Reddick was being brisk with her, but she remaining upbeat, determined not to let anything ruin her day. "It's the end of the month. I bet they could use a hand."

"I think not." Turning her nose up in the air, she flapped her hands like a bald eagle taking flight. "Have a seat in the waiting area. Mr. Morretti will be here any minute."

Before Jariah could respond, Mrs. Reddick walked off.

Releasing a deep sigh, she returned to the couch and sat down. Jariah was bored and growing impatient, but she had no choice but to wait for Nicco to arrive. She retrieved her cell phone from her purse and punched in her password. Jariah had a new text message from her supervisor at Premier Fitness, informing her that her Saturday morning aerobics class was canceled, but it was the message from Wesley's mother that set her teeth on edge.

"Please have my granddaughter dressed and ready to go at five o'clock sharp. We are having dinner at the country club tonight, so ensure that her attire is semiformal."

Jariah's first thought was to call Mrs. Covington and ask her if she was out of her damn mind, but decided against it. On her lunch break, she'd call Stella and explain why Ava was not available tonight. She'd promised her daughter they could go back-to-school shopping, and then grab a bite at Chuck E. Cheese's. And if Jariah canceled her and Ava's plans, her daughter would throw a divalike tantrum.

"Good morning, Jariah. Sorry to keep you waiting."

Feeling guilty for getting caught on her phone, she hurled her BlackBerry into her leather handbag and surged to her feet. She parted her lips to greet her new boss, but when her eyes fell across Nicco's face the word got stuck in her throat. His hair was a mass of loose curls, he smelled like baby powder, and his gaze was so crippling, Jariah couldn't move. In his navy open-collar dress shirt, and tailored white slacks, he would be a shoo-in for a role on the television show *Hawaii Five-O*.

"Are you okay? You look upset."

Nicco gave her arm a light squeeze. His touch made her hot in places that made her blush, and sent her hormones into overdrive. "Me, upset? No, I'm fine. Great actually."

Jariah vigorously nodded her head, pretended everything was A-OK, but it wasn't. Not by a long shot. Nicco had impeccable swag, a unique style all his own, and she was hopelessly attracted to him. Damn it. And her body was sending mixed signals to her brain. She was breathing hard, and her heartbeat was pounding in her ears. Nicco had a strong presence, and confidence to spare, and his tender caress filled her with a deep, aching longing. *He's just a man. You can do this. Keep it together.*

"I love the cut of your dress, and the color looks incredible on you."

Incredible? Really? Pleased, Jariah touched the pearl necklace she'd paired with her turquoise wrap-style dress.

"How about we kick off the day with a tour?"

"That would be great." Jariah opened her purse, and took out a pen and notebook. "Lead the way. I'm right behind you."

Nicco frowned. "What's with the Sherlock kit?"

"I'm horrible with names, and I don't want to offend anyone, so I figured I'd take notes of all the key players in each department."

"Ingenious. I'm already impressed."

Taking her by the arm, he led her through the lobby and into the waiting elevator.

For the next hour, Nicco escorted Jariah to each department and introduced her to his staff. At the end of the tour and the impromptu meet-and-greet, they returned to his tenth-floor office. Larger than a high-school gymnasium, it was filled with books, collectible airplanes and more electronic gadgets than the Apple Store. Framed photographs of Nicco at various sporting events with his celebrity friends and at famous monuments covered the walls. The chocolate-brown decor was striking, and the leather furniture, modern lights and vintage movie posters created a laid-back feel. The windows were open, infusing the office with sunshine, and warmth, but the air held the faint scent of tobacco.

"What's your impression of my company?" Nicco leaned against his white, lacquer desk and crossed his legs at the ankles. "Do you think you'll be happy working here?"

"Absolutely," Jariah said, unable to hide her excitement. Her first day was off to a great start, and she couldn't wait to go home and tell her girlfriends about all of the amazing employee perks at the multi-million dollar company. "Everyone's been incredibly kind, and your staff room is so cozy that I may never go home!"

"Fine by me. I often work late into the night, and I could use the company."

His words and the grin that shaped his mouth were filled with sexual innuendo. To stop herself from making googly eyes at him, Jariah flipped open her notebook and scanned her notes. "I was hoping to meet your vice president, Tye Caldwell. Is he here today?"

Nicco crossed his arms. "What do you know about Tye?"

There was a bitter edge in his tone that surprised her.

"I was doing some research on Morretti Inc. last night, and found the article you did for *Eminence* magazine back in 2001," she explained. "Is it true that you met Mr. Caldwell during a stint in juvy when you were both sixteen?"

"Yes, unfortunately it is. Tye grew up on the wrong side of the tracks, and I was a spoiled rich kid with a chip on my shoulder, but the moment we met we clicked," he said with a fond look in his eyes. "We partied, chased girls and ripped and ran the streets together for years."

"It sounds like you two have a tight bond."

Sadness flickered in his eyes, but he straightened to his full height and tapped his wristwatch. "How about some lunch? I'm hungry and I bet you are, too."

"Lunch? But I haven't done anything yet."

"You've done plenty," he insisted. "I like the way you handled yourself with the department heads. They're great guys, but they can be rude and curt sometimes. Don't let them get away with it."

"Duly noted." Jariah dropped her notebook in her purse and zipped it up. "If it's okay with you, I'd like to see my office and get settled in before I take my coffee break."

"Your office?" He extended his hands to his sides. "You're standing in it."

Completely floored, all Jariah could do was stare wide-eyed at her new boss. She struggled with her words, and foolishly said the first thing that came to mind. "Are you serious?"

Nicco grinned.

"You expect me to work here, with you, all day long?"

"Absolutely. After all, you *are my* executive assistant."

He gestured across the room, and Jariah reluctantly followed the route of his gaze. An L-shaped desk and matching swivel chair was positioned beside the far wall. Next to the computer was a vintage lamp, an iPad, a leather-bound agenda and a glass vase overflowing with long-stemmed yellow roses. "I thought I'd be out front in reception."

"Why? You're a vital part of this company, and I need you close at hand at all times."

"I can't work in here," she blurted out. Jariah could

feel the tension in the air, and saw the challenge in Nicco's eyes. "You smoke, and the smell of tobacco makes me queasy. How can I do my job effectively if I'm nauseous every day?"

"I'm not a smoker." Nicco thought for a moment, then shrugged and said, "Sometimes, when I'm stressed, I like to fire up a cigar, but now that I know it bothers you I'll stop."

"You will? Just like that? Cold turkey?"

"You have my word. This is your office, too, and I want you to feel comfortable."

Nicco's words blindsided her. He was reputed to be one of the most charming bachelors in Miami, and now Jariah could see why. He made her feel special, made her think he cared. But still, her doubts persisted and grew with each second that ticked off the wall clock, so Jariah asked the question circling her brain. "What are you going to do the next time you're stressed out?"

His eyes zeroed in on her face. "Sit back and enjoy the view."

"You're right. This is an amazing view of the Miami skyline," Jariah said, moving toward the window. It was another clear, summer day, and seeing the deep blue sky had a calming effect on her. "Okay, I'm ready to get started. What would you like me to tackle first?"

"Lunch!" Nicco patted his stomach. "I'm starving, woman!"

Jariah laughed. "Would you like me to order something from one of the nearby cafés?"

"My restaurant provides lunch for all Morretti Inc. employees, but since today is your first day I've arranged something extra special for you."

"You have?"

"I made reservations for us at Casa Tua. Do you like it there?"

Like it there? Hell, I've never even heard of the place!

"Maybe if we're lucky we'll run into the cast of *Dating in the City*," he continued. "They're in town filming their season finale, and they paid a visit to Dolce Vita last night."

"You don't have to take me out for lunch. It's really not necessary—"

"I think it is," Nicco said firmly. "You joined the Morretti Inc. family, and that's definitely worth celebrating. Let's go enjoy a great meal and get to know each other better."

His sensual tone made her temperature soar. Jariah was experiencing emotions that were foreign to her, desires she had no business feeling. Not about her new boss, anyway. "I'm not hungry," she lied, ignoring her hunger pangs. "I'll just grab something from the vending machine later."

"First, you ditch me at my restaurant, and now you're giving me a hard time about taking you out for lunch. Do you have a problem being seen with me in public?"

Jariah dropped her gaze to the floor. "No, of course not, but I have a one o'clock meeting with Mrs. Reddick, and I'm worried we won't be back in time."

"Trust me, Mrs. Reddick won't mind if you're a few minutes late."

"Maybe not, but it's important to me to me to be punctual and prepared. My dad always said it's better to be an hour early than a minute late, and it's a motto I live by."

His scowl faded. "Your father sounds like a wise man. I look forward to meeting him."

Confused, she looked at him inquiringly. *Come again?*

"I'll call Mrs. Reddick from the car and give her a heads up. Sound good?"

"I guess that would be okay."

"Of course it's okay. I'm the boss, remember?"

Gesturing to the door, Nicco scooped his keys off his desk and hustled Jariah back through his office. In the reception area, he stopped to give instructions to his secretary and checked the day's mail. Jariah felt uncomfortable with the hand Nicco had on her back, but what made her break out into a cold sweat were the murderous glares she received from the other female employees in the lobby.

Chapter 8

Jariah popped a breath mint into her mouth, slapped a smile on her face and knocked on the open door at the end of the hallway on the ninth floor. The office was spotless, and furnished with oil paintings and scrumptious furniture.

"Good afternoon, Mrs. Reddick. I'm here for my employee orientation. Is now a good time or would you like me to come back?"

"You're late," she said coolly, not bothering to look up from the document she was reading. "I was expecting you an hour ago."

"Mr. Morretti pushed back our meeting. Didn't you get the message?"

Mrs. Reddick whipped off her eyeglasses and dropped them on her desk. "I don't appreciate the last-minute notice, or having to rearrange my schedule for you, either."

Then take it up with the boss, not me, Jariah thought, but didn't dare say.

"Come in and close the door behind you."

Her tone was sharp, but Jariah didn't take offense. She was in a great mood, feeling as light and carefree as a ballerina gliding across the stage. And for the first time in months she was hopeful about her future. She'd had a long, relaxing lunch with Nicco, and learned some surprising information about her new, Italian-born boss. He spoke three languages, had traveled to more than fifty countries and was a die-hard sports fan. The biggest shock of all? He coached Little League Soccer, and mentored at-risk youth. Nicco Morretti was a walking, talking contradiction, and when they finally left Casa Tua two hours later, Jariah realized that there was more to the CEO than met the eye. And that intrigued her.

"I said come in and sit down."

Startled, Jariah blinked, and snapped out of her thoughts. Commanding her legs to move, she strode inside the office and took a seat at one of the brown arm chairs in front of the desk.

"I need to ask you a few questions." Mrs. Reddick sat up taller and clasped her hands together. "Why did you take the executive assistant job?"

"Because Morretti Incorporated is a successful, innovative company with countless opportunities for personal and professional growth."

"And," she pressed, leaning forward in her leather, swivel chair.

"And because I know I have what it takes to be a top-notch executive assistant."

"You expect me to believe that your attraction to Mr. Morretti had nothing to do with it?"

Jariah felt her eyes pop and her mouth sag open.

"The only reason you took the job is to get close to Nicco, isn't it?"

"Excuse me?"

Mrs. Reddick leveled a finger at her. "Don't play dumb with me, Ms. Brooks. I see the way you look at him, and more importantly how he looks at you."

Her words shocked Jariah, causing adrenaline and desire to flare inside the walls of her chest. So what? She was attracted to Nicco. Big deal. It didn't mean she was going to sleep with him or do anything to jeopardize her new job. That's why instead of coming clean, Jariah furrowed her eyebrows and wore a confused face. "I'm afraid I don't know what you're talking about."

"I think you do," she shot back. "I'm onto you, Ms. Brooks. I know what you're after."

Perspiration drenched Jariah's skin, and a cold shiver ripped through her body. She couldn't think and the room was spinning on its head. The walls were closing in, and the office suddenly felt smaller than an airplane bathroom. Jariah struggled to kept her composure. Lashing out would get her nowhere, and she had no intention of losing her job on the first day.

"I don't believe in beating around the bush, so I'm going to get straight to the point."

The HR director's icy tone put her on edge. Jariah wanted to storm out of the office and slam the door so hard the windows shattered, but she didn't want Mrs. Reddick to know she'd gotten under her skin.

"Mr. Morretti hired you for one reason, and one reason only, and that's to get you into bed."

Jariah swallowed a gasp. Her heartbeat pounded in her ears like a jackhammer. At the thought of making love to Nicco—a man she shared amazing chemistry with—blood rushed straight to her core. Her breasts swelled, and her nipples hardened under her dress.

Flustered, Jariah wet her lips with her tongue, and breathed deeply through her nose. Her thoughts cleared, but her burning desire for her new boss remained.

"It's obvious you're taken with Mr. Morretti, and he with you, so I thought it was important to have an honest talk with you."

"I'm not taken with anyone, Mrs. Reddick."

Her oval-shaped eyes were pools of blue, and filled with skepticism. "As I was saying, I hired you to assist Mr. Morretti in his day-to-day affairs, not to seduce him, and I won't tolerate any hanky-panky at this company."

Hanky panky? You've got *to be kidding me!* Jariah bit the inside of her cheek to keep from laughing out loud. Her legs stopped shaking, and for the first time since arriving at Mrs. Reddick's office Jariah felt herself relax and her confidence return.

"Mr. Morretti is a smooth talker who loves female attention," she explained with the air and expertise of a trained psychologist. "He flirts with everyone, so don't think you're special. You're simply one of many. Furthermore, he's never been a one-woman man and is dead-set against ever getting married."

Annoyed, Jariah struggled to control her temper. *Does she warn every new female employee about Nicco? Or did she tailor-make this speech just for me?*

"I know a lot of people in the financial sector, and if I find out in the future you had an inappropriate relationship with Mr. Morretti, you'll never work in this town again."

Jariah gripped the arms of her chair. She didn't want to get into a screaming match with Mrs. Reddick, but she had to make it clear where she stood on office romances. "I have years of work experience under my belt, and a résumé I'm incredibly proud of," she began, though her tone was free of pride. "I have never been inappropriate with a colleague, and I have no intention of having an affair with anyone at this company."

Mrs. Reddick raised her eyebrows in a questioning slant, but didn't speak. The phone rang, but she ignored it and continued staring Jariah down as if she were a common criminal.

"Mr. Morretti and I will have an employer-employee

relationship and nothing more. I'm not here to find a husband, Mrs. Reddick. I'm here to advance my career."

"I won't let you or anyone else bring shame to this fine company again, and if…"

Again? The word rattled around Jariah's head, rousing her curiosity. *What had Nicco done?* she wondered. *And more importantly, what the hell have I gotten myself into?*

"Don't indulge Mr. Morretti," Mrs. Reddick continued, raising her voice above the noise and animated conversations streaming through the office walls. "Do your work and remain professional at all times. Have I made myself clear?"

"Like crystal," Jariah said tightly, her jaw stiff and her teeth clenched.

"I'll be watching you." Mrs. Reddick opened her bottom drawer, pulled out a large manila envelope and slammed the drawer shut. "Read through the employee handbook and don't forget to date and sign your contract. Make yourself a copy and put the original in my mailbox."

"What about my employee orientation?"

Mrs. Reddick pushed the envelope across the desk. "We just had it."

"But I have questions about the benefits package and the upcoming training sessions."

"Then read the employee handbook. It covers everything, but if you still have—"

A female voice floated over the intercom, causing the HR director to trail off.

"Sorry to interrupt but Mr. Morretti Sr. is on line one," she said in an urgent tone. "I told him you were in a meeting, but he demanded I put his call through."

Sweat glistened on Mrs. Reddick's forehead, and panic filled her eyes. "That's all for now." She made a shooing motion with one hand and snatched up the phone receiver with the other. "Please close the door on your way out."

Standing, Jariah scooped up the envelope and thanked Mrs. Reddick for her time. As she exited the office, she overhead the HR director say, "You have nothing to worry about, Arturo. I just spoke to Ms. Brooks. Trust me, she isn't going to be a problem…"

Outside in the hallway, Jariah slumped against the wall. She needed a moment to make sense of what just happened. The HR director was a know-it-all, the type of woman who liked throwing her weight around, in essence, a bully in a Chanel suit. Jariah wondered what Nicco would think about the disparaging things Mrs. Reddick had said about him. Her brain was hazy, but she remembered every detail of her conversation with Mrs. Reddick.

I see the way you look at him, and more importantly how he looks at you… Mr. Morretti hired you for one reason, and one reason only and that's to get you into bed.

Jariah banished the thought from her mind, straightened and strode purposefully down the wide, bright corridor. No one was going to intimidate her, or push her around. She was going to prove her ingenuity, and by the time she found an account manager job and quit Morretti Incorporated, Nicco would be singing her praises. And not because she'd slept with him but because she'd worked her ass off.

Sleeping with him to advance her career was a ludicrous notion, one she would never consider. It wasn't going to happen. Ever. No way.

Jariah spotted Nicco exiting the staff room surrounded by a bevy of young, wide-eyed interns, and felt her gaze slide down his broad, sinfully sexy physique. Their eyes met, and her world stopped. His face brightened, and a devilish grin curled his full, juicy lips.

Jariah clutched the envelope tightly to her chest. To her surprise, he turned away from his adoring group and headed straight toward her. Her heart fluttered with nervous anticipation. His footsteps pounded on the floor, and his expensive cologne wafted through the air, seizing every woman's attention on the ninth floor.

Butterflies swarmed her belly, danced and fluttered earnestly. In her mind, she imagined herself kissing and caressing Nicco's lean, chiseled face, and quickly deleted the thought. Advancing her career was all that mattered. Tonight she was going to educate herself about the company, and come Monday morning she'd be up to speed.

"How did your employee orientation go?"

Trust me, you don't want to know. "It was great," she lied, glancing over her shoulder to ensure Mrs. Reddick wasn't spying on them. Jariah wouldn't put anything past the HR director, and as she followed him to the elevators, she made a mental note to keep Nicco's office door open at all times. Being alone with him was too risky; there was too much temptation. The last thing Jariah wanted was to give her colleagues—especially the female staff—the wrong impression. "Mrs. Reddick is a wealth of useful information, and I learned a lot from her."

"I'm glad to hear it."

Inside the elevator, they discussed his schedule, his upcoming business trip to Los Angeles, and the anniversary party he was throwing for his parents next month. He spoke about his parents with love and affection, and Jariah found herself overcome with sadness and longing. She wanted to make things right with her mom and dad, but didn't know how. They'd been estranged for months, and she missed them dearly.

When they reached tenth floor, Jariah noticed it was dead quiet and that all of the offices were empty. "Where is everyone?" she asked as they approached the reception area. "This place looks like a ghost town."

"On Fridays, employees only work half days," he explained, cocking an eyebrow. "Didn't Mrs. Reddick mention that during your employee orientation?"

"I, um, must have forgotten."

"No worries, Jariah. It's you're first day, and you've been bombarded with information."

He pulled back the sleeve of his dress shirt and checked his gold wristwatch. "It's already three o'clock. You better get going or you'll get stuck in rush hour on your way home."

"Are you sure? I don't mind sticking around a little longer."

"There's no point. I'll be heading out shortly, and everyone else is gone for the day."

"You must have a hot date tonight." Jariah heard the question spring out of her loose lips, and wished she could stuff them back inside her big, fat mouth. *What is the matter with you? Do you want Mrs. Reddick to march in here and bitch slap you?*

"What I meant to say was, you must have a busy weekend planned with your friends."

"Yeah, tonight I'm hanging out with my godson, and on Sunday my boys and I will be at Gulfstream Park." Nicco wore a curious expression. "Do you like thoroughbred racing?"

"The sport of kings is a little too rich for my blood. I'm more of a fly-fishing girl."

Amusement lit his eyes. "Fly-fishing, huh?"

"My dad taught me everything there is to know about the sport."

"I've always wanted to learn. Maybe you can teach me one day."

And earn Mrs. Reddick's wrath? No way!

"Why don't you bring some of your girlfriends and join me in my luxury box?" Nicco proposed. "The food is outstanding, the view is spectacular, and the park will be crawling with celebs. It's a guaranteed good time."

"Thanks for the invitation, but I have plans with my

daughter." *Eating junk food and watching Disney movies is hardly exciting, but I'm a homebody at heart, and I love the idea of spending quality time with my baby girl.*

Rap music filled the air. "That's my personal cell," Nicco said, glancing inside his office. "Have a good weekend, Jariah. See you on, Monday."

"Thanks, you, too. Good luck on the race track."

Jariah scooped up her handbag and walked down the hallway, feeling better than she had in weeks. Finally, things were going her way, and if she kept her attraction to Nicco quiet and found a way to avoid Mrs. Reddick, life would be perfect.

Chapter 9

Noise, laughter and squeals of delight filled the Chuck
E. Cheese's on Biscayne Boulevard, and as Jariah entered
the family-friendly restaurant with Ava, she noticed every
booth in the seating area was occupied. The center was
crowded, and children raced around bumping into each
other and everything that got in their way.

The scent of corn dogs and cheese pizza stirred Jariah's
hunger, making her mouth water and her stomach grum-
ble. Walking around Aventura mall for hours, trying on
shoes and clothes with a temperamental six-year-old was
exhausting, and all Jariah wanted now was a cold drink
and a place to rest her aching feet. Inside her tote bag was
the employee package, the Morretti Incorporated summer
report and a copy of Nicco's August schedule. Her plan
was to read while Ava played, and when Jariah spotted a
family of three vacate their booth, she rushed across the
room and dumped her things on the table.

"Mom, can I go to the kid's zone?" Ava asked.

"You have an hour to play, and that's it." Jariah helped
her daughter out of her purple raincoat and chucked it on
the seat. "And no running. I don't want you to get hurt."

Ava stuck out her hand and wiggled her fingers. "Mom, I need some money for tokens."

Jariah reached inside her tote bag and gave Ava five dollars.

"That's it? Dad usually gives me twenty bucks."

"Is that before or after you throw a hissy fit?"

"I need more money."

Reluctantly, Jariah opened her wallet. Ava snatched a ten-dollar bill, and took off like a rocket into the games and arcade section.

Jariah sat down in the booth, and got down to work. What she read in the employee package fascinated her. Morretti Incorporated was one of the leading players in the shipping industry, but it was their investment division, which was headed up by Nicco, that was growing in leaps and bounds. Since opening Dolce Vita in 2004, the charismatic CEO had used his charm and connections to shoot up the celebrity stratosphere. In ten short years, he'd built a multi-million-dollar empire comprised of five-star restaurants, trendy cafés and endorsement and sponsorship deals. But what impressed Jariah most of all about the family-owned company was their commitment to charity work and their employee-friendly work environment.

"Are you ready to go down, chump?"

"Bring it on, Uncle Nicco. I'm not scared of you!"

Frowning with her yellow highlighter suspended in mid-air, Jariah glanced around in search of the familiar voice. And there, at the arcade basketball game was Nicco and a small boy with glasses. Amused, Jariah watched them play, and laughed when Nicco threw his hands up in victory. Nicco did the moonwalk around the pinball machine, and the kid—and everyone standing nearby— cracked up.

Unable to resist teasing her boss, Jariah slid out of the booth and joined the pair at the arcade basketball game. "No one likes a show-off," she said, shaking her head in disapproval. "I think you owe your opponent an apology *and* something from the concession stand."

"Jariah, what are you doing here?" Nicco folded his arms as if he was upset, but a grin was playing on his lips. "Are you stalking me?"

"You wish!" she quipped, her tone full of sass.

"Now, is that anyway to talk to the man who'll be signing your paychecks?"

Shame burned her cheeks. "You're right. I am so sorry. I wasn't thinking—"

"Relax, Jariah. I was only kidding."

His touch to her forearm was warm and gentle. "This handsome kid with the killer jump shot is my godson," he said, ruffling the kid's hair. "Richie, say hello to Ms. Brooks."

"You're pretty," the boy gushed, his eyes bright. "Do you have a man?"

Surprised by the question and the child's obvious confidence, Jariah gave Nicco a pointed look. "You put him up to that, didn't you?"

"I did no such thing." Nicco raised his hands in the air, like a fugitive surrendering to the police. "He's a smart kid. He knows a quality woman when he sees one."

"So, now you're his wingman?"

Nicco threw his head back and chuckled long and hard.

"Mom!" Ava ran over, her pigtails flapping in the air and her face covered with excitement. "I need more money. Can I have twenty bucks?"

"No, I just gave you ten dollars."

Nicco took out his wallet and handed Ava a fifty-dollar bill. "Here you go, Ava. Knock yourself out."

"Wow." Her mouth agape, Ava stared intently at the bill, as if her big, brown eyes were deceiving her. "Thank you, mister!"

Jariah shook her head. "Nicco, that's too much money. She's only six-years-old."

"Let her have some fun," he said with a wink.

Ava danced around in circles. "Yippee! Now, I can play 'Western Wrangler'!"

"You like that game?" Richie wiggled his eyebrows. "But you're a girl."

"So, what?" Ava sassed. "I'm good at it. I bet I can beat you."

"Bring it on!"

The children took off running and made a beeline for the "Western Wrangler" machine.

"Thanks a lot, Nicco. Now, I'll *never* see my daughter again!"

"Or you can look at it as an opportunity to schmooze with your new boss."

"I must admit," Jariah said, dodging his heated gaze, "I'm surprised to see you here."

"I don't know why." Mischief twinkled in his eyes and his mouth held a teasing smile. "I've been coming here since I was Richie's age, and the only thing I like more than arcade games is playing 'Dance Dance Revolution' on my Wii."

Jariah giggled. To her friends and family she was Ms. Independent—a serious, no-nonsense woman who didn't have time to play. But deep down she longed to be with someone fun, lively and energetic, and found herself wishing Nicco was anyone *but* her boss.

"Let's order some snacks," Nicco said, gesturing to the concession stand. "The kids will be starving once their tokens run out, and I don't want to feel your daughter's wrath."

"We can share a booth. There's more than enough room at mine."

"That's great. I'll go get the snacks and meet you there."

Ten minutes later, Nicco returned carrying two trays filled with junk food.

"How much do I owe you?" Jariah asked, reaching for her purse.

"Put your money away. It's my treat."

"I'd like to pay my share."

"Too bad," he said, settling into the booth. "Your money's no good here."

Dismissing his words, she took out a twenty-dollar bill out of her wallet and slid it across the table. "Thanks again for grabbing this stuff. Everything looks delicious."

"Are you always this difficult?"

Jariah didn't know what to say, so she smiled.

"Keep your cash. Or better yet, give it to Ava so she can buy more tokens." Nicco picked up the money, tucked it back inside Jariah's purse and gestured to the manila envelope. "You brought work with you to Chuck E. Cheese's? Why? You're supposed to be having fun with your daughter, not memorizing the employee handbook."

"I know, but next week is going to be extremely busy, and I want to be prepared. I have a lot to learn, and I don't want to embarrass myself during the Monday morning staff meeting."

He plucked a piece of cheesy bread out of the wicker basket and took a healthy bite. "I don't expect you to know everything about Morretti Incorporated overnight. It's going to take time for you to learn the ins and outs of the company. As long as you're driven and hardworking, we'll get along fine."

"Thank God." Releasing a sigh of relief, Jariah wiped imaginary sweat from her brow. "I was worried I'd get canned if I couldn't recite the company mission statement by Monday!"

The lively atmosphere inside Chuck E. Cheese's helped Jariah relax, and soon she was laughing at Nicco's jokes and cracking some of her own. As they ate, they chatted about their families, the upcoming Kings of R & B concert, and their mutual love of romantic comedies.

"What's your all-time favorite movie?"

"That's an easy one," Jariah said without missing a beat. *"Poetic Justice."*

"Back in the day you had a thing for Tupac Shakur, didn't you?"

"Everyone did!" she quipped, laughing. "I've seen it a million times, and I still love Tupac!"

A dimple appeared in his cheek when he chuckled. Leaning forward, he rested his elbows casually on the table. "Do you and your ex have a good relationship?"

"Yeah, for the most part." Jariah searched the arcade for Ava, and when she found her precocious daughter at the "Pac Man" machine she thought her heart would burst with love. "Ava means the world to us and at the end of the day that's all that matters."

"Are you guys done for good or trying to work things out for your daughter's sake?"

"That ship sailed and sank a long time ago. We're definitely over."

"And you're not dating anyone right now? I find that hard to believe."

He had a hungry, predatory look in his eyes, one that caused her body to tingle and vibrate in a hundred different places. It was times like this, when Nicco was flirting with her, that she forgot he was one of the most successful restaurateurs in the country—and her boss. "You ask a lot of personal questions."

"I don't mean anything by it. I just want to get to know you better. I figure learning more about you and your beautiful daughter is a great place to start.

"It's your turn," Nicco said, draping his hands casually along the back of their booth. "Go ahead. Ask me anything."

Reaching for her glass of lemonade, Jariah tried to recall everything she'd read online about Nicco. "Is it true you dated three *Sports Illustrated* models at the same time?"

Jariah expected him to laugh or flash a bad-boy grin, but he didn't. He looked embarrassed, not proud, and his eyes darkened with regret. "That was a long time ago, back when I had more money than sense. I was twenty-five, new to Miami and thought I was 'the man.'"

"And now?"

"And now I'm older, wiser and smarter about relationships," he replied quietly. "I recently met a woman I'm completely smitten with and I'm not afraid to pursue her."

Jariah sat perfectly still. She didn't want Nicco to know his words had excited her, or that she craved his touch. Just the thought of his strong, masculine hands caressing her flesh shot a fiery rush of desire down her spine.

"Cheese pizza! Yay, my favorite!"

Jariah blinked and gave her head a hard shake. It didn't help, but she turned away from Nicco and focused on her daughter. Patting the seat beside her, she smiled and kissed Ava on the forehead. "Hey, sweetie. Did you have fun playing in the arcade with Richie?"

"I beat him twice, Mom!"

"No, only once," Richie argued. "The second time I let you win."

Everyone at the table laughed.

"Are you my mom's new boyfriend?" Ava asked, facing Nicco. "My mom dumped my dad because he wouldn't marry her. Are you going to marry her and become my stepdad?"

Jariah was mortified, but waved a hand in the air, as if her daughter's question was no big deal. But it was. She didn't want Nicco to think—not even for a second—that she was interested in him. According to Mrs. Reddick, he liked to screw the help, and Jariah had no intention of becoming his office plaything.

"I'm your mom's new boss, Ava, and she's doing a fantastic job," Nicco said in a sincere tone. "You should be very proud of her."

"Way to go, Mom!" Ava cheered. "Can you give my mom a raise so she can take me to Disneyland for Christmas?"

Jariah cupped a hand over her daughter's mouth, and gestured to her half-eaten plate of food. "Ava, leave Mr. Morretti alone and finish eating your pizza."

"I love Disneyland." Richie licked barbecue sauce off his fingers. "Uncle Nicco takes me and my mom to California every year. Maybe you guys can come, too."

"I like the way you think. The more the merrier, right?"

"Right, Uncle Nicco, and we can take your RV!"

Jariah raised her eyebrows. "You have an RV?"

"I sure do." He wore a proud smile, as if he'd built the recreational vehicle with his bare hands. "I've racked up thousands of miles since buying my Platinum Plus RV last year, and I have plans to drive to Disneyland for Thanksgiving. Are you and Ava free?"

"We're free!" Ava chirped, eagerly clapping her hands. "Wait until I tell the kids at day camp I'm going to Disneyland. They're going to be *so* jealous!"

"Nicco, you can't be serious. We can't go with you to Anaheim."

"Why not? There's plenty of room, and I'm absorbing the costs."

"I started at Morretti Incorporated this morning," she pointed out, blown away by his outrageous offer. "I don't even know how you take your coffee."

He winked. "I don't. I prefer to start my day off with a banana and a glass of O.J."

"Uncle Nicco, can we play another round of hoops before we go?" Richie guzzled down his apple juice and jumped to his feet. "I'm feeling lucky, and I know I can win this time."

"Sure. What about you, Ava? Are you up for a game of one-on-one?"

Jariah spoke up. "Not tonight. We have to get going. It's almost nine o'clock."

"But I don't want to go," Ava whined, folding her arms. "I want to play basketball."

An awkward silence fell across the table.

"Ava, be a good girl for your mom, and next week you can come with us to Boomers."

Ava's frown disappeared. "All right. I'll behave." She stood and put on her raincoat. "I love Boomers. I'm great at miniature golf, but I'll let you guys win when we play, okay?"

"You're going down," Nicco vowed. "I'm the king of miniature golf. Tell her, Richie…"

A moment passed before Jariah realized Nicco had not only diffused the situation, but he'd also brightened her daughter's mood. She was chatting excitedly and laughing at Richie's jokes. He definitely had a way with kids, and although Jariah would never bribe Ava, she appreciated him making the effort to connect with her daughter.

"Thanks for everything, Nicco. I'll see you on Monday morning."

"You can bet on it," he said, standing. "Good night, ladies."

Quickly, Jariah collected her things, waved goodbye and hustled Ava back through the play center. Ten minutes later, they were on the I-95, listening to the radio. Her conversation with Nicco filled her mind. It turned out she'd pegged him all wrong. He loved the ladies—no doubt about it—but he was laugh-out-loud funny, had a weak spot for kids and was incredibly generous. *Shoot, if I can survive living with my ex, I can definitely handle a pretty-boy CEO who loves kids, junk food and arcade games!*

Chapter 10

August was a whirlwind of business meetings, visits to Dolce Vita and laughs shared between Nicco and Jariah during coffee breaks, long, relaxing lunches and after-work drinks. Although she'd been working at Morretti Incorporated for weeks, Jariah still couldn't believe she was being paid to attend industry events, to socialize with foreign clients and to schmooze with celebrities. As she unlocked Nicco's office door on Friday morning, she decided taking the executive assistant position had been one of the smartest decisions she'd ever made.

Opening the blinds, Jariah stood in front of the window, soaking in the early-morning sunshine. She stared at the sky and admired the peaceful, tranquil view of downtown Miami. The streets were surprisingly quiet; traffic flowed smoothly in and out of the core, and casually dressed people wearing shades and clutching coffee cups strolled through the business district.

Remembering she had a full day ahead of her, Jariah hung her jacket on the coat rack and got down to business. At her desk, she flipped through the mail she'd collected from the administration office, anxious to find her first paycheck. It was on the bottom of the pile, and when Jariah ripped open the envelope her eyes froze on the check. Several seconds passed, but her mouth remained wide-open. Someone in accounting had made a mistake, and although Jariah could use the extra nine hundred dollars she knew keeping the money would be wrong.

Jariah dialed the extension for the financial administrator, and when prompted left a detailed message. The moment she put down the receiver her cell phone buzzed. It was Nicco texting her to find out what she wanted to eat for breakfast. Every day, he arrived at the office with the most delicious foods, and although Jariah would never admit it, their morning talks were the highlight of her day. Jariah read the text, and her heart swooned.

Beautiful, I have a surprise for you. See you in a few minutes.

Excitement radiated throughout Jariah's body, but she warned herself to relax. Just because Nicco showered her with compliments and did sweet, thoughtful things for her every day didn't mean they were soul mates. They weren't. She had Ava, and he had a harem of lovers, and no matter how much she desired him, they could never be more than colleagues.

Mrs. Reddick's words came back in a rush, flooding her mind.

Mr. Morretti is a smooth talker who flirts with everyone, so don't think you're special. Furthermore, he's dead-set against ever getting married...

Jariah shook off her thoughts, but the HR director's voice echoed in her head like a bullhorn. *You're simply one of many...* A scowl curled her lips. Funny, but in the past few weeks, she hadn't seen Nicco put the moves on anyone. Not a hostess, not a waitress, not even the attractive soap star who'd pounced on him yesterday at Dolce Vita.

Hearing her desk phone buzz, she picked it up and hit

line one. "Good morning. This is Ms. Brooks, executive assistant to Nicco Morretti. How many I help you?"

"I'm sorry," a woman with a low, throaty voice said. "But I didn't catch your name."

"It's Jariah. Who may I ask is calling?"

"It's Vivica Morretti, Nicco's mother. Is my son around?"

"No, not yet, but I'm expecting him any minute now."

Mrs. Morretti released a long, deep sigh. "That boy is never going to change. He arrived two weeks *after* my due date, and has been late ever since!"

Jariah swallowed a laugh.

"You sound awfully young, Ms. Brooks. Just how old are you?"

"I'm twenty-seven."

"Of course you are." Mrs. Morretti sounded exasperated, like a customer waiting in a slow-moving line at the bank. "Are you sleeping with my son? Is that why he hired you?"

A cold shiver tore through her. *Why do people keep interrogating me about Nicco? Why is our relationship suddenly on everyone's mind?* Last night at dinner, Sadie and Felicia had questioned her relentlessly, and now Mrs. Morretti—a woman she'd never met—was in her business. Jariah actually considered disconnecting the phone, but instead spoke in a firm, strong voice. "No, Mrs. Morretti, I'm not. I don't believe in mixing business with pleasure, and furthermore I'm here to serve the needs of the Morretti Incorporated, not your son."

"And that's the truth?"

"Absolutely. I want to advance my career, not ruin my reputation."

"Good answer," she said, her tone warmer, brighter. "I look forward to meeting you, Ms. Brooks. Will you be at my anniversary bash?"

For the second time in minutes, Jariah's eyes widened.

"You know about the surprise party? How? Nicco has gone to great lengths to ensure you don't find out."

"I know, isn't that cute? My sons and my husband think I'm completely in the dark about the surprise party, but I knew about the anniversary bash before *they* did!" Mrs. Morretti's loud, feverish laughter floated over the line. "I raised three troublesome boys and helped my husband get his business off the ground. Nothing *ever* gets past me."

"Nicco's going to be crushed when he finds out you know about the surprise party."

"That's why we're not going to tell him, right, Ms. Brooks?"

"Right," she said with a nod of her head. "I won't say a word."

"I have to run. I have a ten o'clock appointment at Le Chic. I haven't found a gown yet, and the anniversary bash is just weeks away."

"Good luck finding the perfect dress."

"I don't need luck," Mrs. Morretti quipped. "I have my husband's platinum card *and* Oprah's stylist along for the ride!"

Laughing, Jariah hung up the phone and turned on her computer.

She was hard at work, answering emails and proof-reading documents, but the moment she heard Nicco out in reception, she grabbed the mirror from inside her bottom drawer and assessed her look. This morning she'd made the time to do her makeup, and loved how her scarlet-red lipstick made her eyes pop and brightened her entire face.

"Sorry I'm late." Nicco stalked over to the sitting area, put the brown paper bag on the glass table and took off his sunglasses. "I stopped to grab us breakfast from Javalicious and the line was ridiculously slow. Ready to eat?"

Jariah sucked in a deep breath at the sight of Nicco dressed in a white, short-sleeve shirt, khaki slacks and leather sandals. Desire rushed through her veins. He was standing on the opposite side of the office, a good ten feet away, but shivers of electricity crackled between them. He looked like an all-American boy but his dark locks and scrumptious grin made him irresistible. That's why, despite the warning from Mrs. Reddick weeks earlier, her gaze crawled all over his toned physique. She wanted to touch him, could almost feel her hands playing in his hair as she stroked his body with her own.

"Nicco, you didn't have to bring me breakfast," she said, wiping her damp palms along the side of her chair. Goose bumps broke out across her skin. Her attraction to Nicco was spiraling out of control, literally turning her into a sex fiend, and Jariah feared what would happen if she acted on her feelings. There was nothing cute about getting axed, and she had no intention of being unemployed again. "I'm not hungry. I had a protein bar on the way here."

"Then consider this a mid-morning snack."

Nicco pulled out one of the padded leather chairs. "Come eat. The food is getting cold."

The air was filled with a yummy, lip-smacking aroma, but Jariah didn't move. Her body was a raging inferno, and she couldn't stop staring at Nicco's mouth. All hell would break loose if he touched her, and Jariah didn't want to put herself in harm's way.

"You go ahead. I'll join you once I finish my to-do list." To prove how busy she was, Jariah swept her hands over the paperwork cluttering her desk. "I have to finish the PowerPoint presentation for your Tuesday-morning meeting, and I have to process your monthly travel and expense reports before I leave at noon."

"Work can wait." He spoke in a stern, authoritative tone. "Now, get over here and sit down before I take you over my knee for insubordination."

His words and his sinfully sexy grin made Jariah weak.

The shaking in her body was uncontrollable, fast and overwhelming, and Nicco hadn't even touched her.

"I'm not going to ask you again."

"Okay, okay, I'm coming." She stood, scooped up her iPad and marched her quivering, horny body over to the sitting area. "While we eat, we can discuss your September schedule."

He released a deep sigh, one that spoke of his frustration. "I hate discussing business when we're eating. You know that."

"But you have a meeting with representatives from the Miami Convention Center next week, and I'm dying to know what it's all about."

His smile was back, shining in full force. "I want Dolce Vita to be the official sponsor of the 2016 Miami Auto Show, so I'm meeting with representatives to get the ball rolling."

"Nicco, that's wonderful! They're going to love you and Dolce Vita." Jariah sat down and rested her iPad on the table. "I've been going to that car show since I was a little girl, and every year it gets bigger and better."

"What do *you* know about exotic sports cars? You drive a death trap," he teased, unloading the food containers from the brown paper bag. "I swear, the next time that monstrosity stalls in the employee parking lot, I'm dousing it in gasoline and striking a match!"

Jariah laughed, feeling the stress and tension in her body recede some.

"La colazione è servita, bello. Scavare in!"

His words, though spoken in jest, made her heart swell with pride. *Breakfast is served, beautiful. Dig in.* Jariah loved when Nicco spoke to her in Italian, and every time he paid her a compliment, a big fat smile exploded across her face. *I'd be fine if he wasn't so dreamy,* she thought, draping a napkin over her lap. *Nicco is one of the funni-*

est, most charming men I've ever met. He'd brought her breakfast from her favorite café, and each scrumptious bite Jariah took of her veggie omelet made her moan inwardly. "This is so good," she gushed, closing her eyes in silent appreciation for chefs everywhere. "You should have Chef Gambro add something like this to the menu for Monday's meeting."

"Menu? There is no menu. I'm having a short, informal meeting with representatives at the convention center," he explained. "And besides, Dolce Vita is a classy, high-end restaurant, not a cheap breakfast joint with two-for-one specials."

"Push back the meeting to noon, invite the representatives to your restaurant and have Chef Gambro prepare some of his famous award-winning entrées." Growing excited, she put down her fork and scooted forward in her chair. "Nicco, give them the whole five-star, fine-dining experience. Spare no expense. Go all-out."

"Jariah, you're an accountant," he reminded her. "You're supposed to be helping me save money, not pressuring me to spend more!"

"Sometimes to make money you have to spend money."

Raising his coffee cup in the air, he gave a slow nod. "Touché, Ms. Brooks. Touché."

"Once Dolce Vita becomes the official sponsor of the 2016 Miami Car Show, and people are lined up down the block at your restaurant, you'll be singing my praises. Just wait and see."

"Too late. I already am."

Jariah held her breath. His words left her speechless, rattled her, and when he reached across the table and took her hand, desire scorched her skin. He stroked her fingers ever so gently, as if she was a fragile piece of glass. His sweet caress kindled her body's fire, and every inch of her flesh was sensitive to his soothing touch.

"I think your idea's brilliant," he announced, his voice a thick, sensual whisper. The huskiness of his tone aroused her, and so did the boyish grin that shaped his lips. "But I'm not surprised. You're one of the most creative, insightful people I've ever met, and I feel fortunate to have you working at Morretti Inc."

It was hard to think, to concentrate when Nicco was stroking her skin, sliding his fingers upward, ever so gently. Jariah blinked, convinced herself she was imagining it. Fantasy or not, she recognized the only way to survive the sensual onslaught was by changing the subject. "While you're at The Wine Cellar, I figured I'd make the necessary arrangements for your upcoming trip to L.A.," she said, ignoring the tremor in her voice and her erratic heartbeat. "Do you want me to book a suite for you at the Hilton or The St. Regis?"

"Jariah, you're coming with me to my eleven o'clock appointment."

"Why? I know nothing about wine."

"I want to find some fresh, new brands to add to Dolce Vita's menu and I'd love if you could help me at the sample tasting." His fingers played along the inside of her wrist, turning her on in the worst possible way. "And while we're there we can select the wine for my parents' anniversary bash."

"I almost forgot. Your mother called about an hour ago."

"I figured she would," he said, shrugging his shoulders. "I talked her ear off about you last night, and now she's anxious to meet you."

"You did? What did you say?"

He leaned forward, moving so close his scent wrapped itself around her like a bear hug. "I told her that you're doing an awesome job keeping me in line, and that you're a strong, independent woman with a great head on her shoulders."

His gaze zoomed in on her face, sliding from her eyes to her lips and way down south.

A telephone buzzed, breaking the silence and their steamy connection.

Jariah surged to her feet and dashed across the room. Her hands were slick with sweat, but she snatched up the receiver and put it to her ear. She thanked the financial administrator for returning her call, promised to be at her office in ten minutes, and hung up the phone.

"Is everything okay?" Standing, a frown marring his features, he regarded her closely. "Don't tell me the accounting department screwed up your first paycheck."

"I'm afraid they did. They paid me for three weeks instead of two."

"So, what's the problem?"

"I was paid for days I didn't work."

"And?" he asked, raising an eyebrow.

"And, it's money I didn't earn. I can't keep it. That would be wrong."

Nicco felt his jaw hit the ground. He knew he was standing there, gawking at Jariah, but he couldn't help it. He wouldn't have been more shocked if a spaceship had landed on his desk, and a Martian had popped out singing Broadway show tunes.

"I'm going down to the accounting department to straighten things out." Jariah grabbed her purse off her desk. "I'll meet you in the lobby in fifteen minutes."

Nicco watched Jariah glide through his office door, looking fly and fabulous in her fitted, short-sleeve dress, and tried not to stare. Tried, and failed, of course. *Who knew perfection came in a curvy, five-foot-nine-inch package?* he thought as his eyes trailed her down the hallway. Her legs went on for miles, and then some, and her wicked shape made his nature rise. Nicco didn't know how long he stood there ogling her, but it felt like an eternity. His thoughts were all over the map, and he still couldn't make sense of what Jariah had said moments earlier.

I was paid for days I didn't work... I can't keep the money... It would be wrong.

Jariah was a beauty, a stone-cold fox that made his blood pressure soar, but he admired her honesty more than anything. He'd been enamored with her from the moment he spotted her at Javalicious, and working side-by-side with her for the past three weeks had only increased his interest. Jariah had a hold on him he just couldn't explain. Amazingly, she wasn't impressed by his wealth, and was so fiercely independent, she balked whenever he spent money on her.

For the first time in his life, Nicco found himself thinking about settling down. He could actually envision himself being in a serious, committed relationship with Jariah, but he didn't have the courage to tell her how he felt about her. What if she rejected him? What would he do if she didn't share his feelings?

Releasing a deep sigh, he dragged a hand down the length of his face. He'd never felt so indecisive, so unsure of himself before. He was one of the most successful restaurateurs in the country, and entrepreneurs paid top dollar to hear him speak at various business conventions and workshops. He'd never flubbed a speech, never once let his nerves get the best of him, so why did the thought of having a heart-to-heart talk with Jariah make him break out in a cold sweat? He wanted to take her out on a date—tonight, tomorrow, hell, any day of the week—but how was he supposed to wine her and dine her when their relationship was strictly business?

An idea came to him in a flash. If he wanted to get Jariah alone, after dark, he'd have to trick her. Lying to her didn't sit well with him, but he had no choice. At least that's what he told himself. Nicco wanted Jariah in his bed, *and* on his arm, and he was going to pull out all the stops to make it happen.

Nicco checked his watch, scooped up the phone and dialed the head of his security division. When the call went to voice mail, he left a message and hung up. Gerald and two other guards were escorting a Portuguese businessman to a high-profile function at noon, and although he trusted his team to get the job done, he wanted to ensure everything ran smoothly. Pocketing his cell, he slipped on his sunglasses and exited his office.

In reception, he gave instructions to his personal secretary. "I'm going to The Wine Cellar. Please forward all calls to my cell phone," he said without breaking his stride. "And have the cleaners tidy my office while I'm out."

Minutes later, Nicco strode through the lobby, searching for Jariah. He spotted her in the waiting area, yakking it up with a short, well-dressed man holding a brown leather briefcase. The muscles in his jaw clenched, and his hands curled into fists. What the hell? Who was Jariah talking to? And why was she laughing at the guy's jokes?

Anxious to reach her, Nicco broke into a jog. By the time he got to the waiting area, the stranger was gone, and Jariah was typing furiously on her cell phone. "Who's the suit?" he asked, keeping his tone calm, casual. "What did he want?"

Jariah wore a girlish smile, one Nicco had never seen cross her face before. He loved the way it lit up her eyes and warmed her skin. *Damn, I have it bad,* he thought. He didn't understand his feelings and told himself to get a grip. He wanted to impress her, not drive her away by acting like a jealous control freak.

"He asked me out for dinner."

Nicco cocked an eyebrow. "And what did you say?"

"I said yes. He's a single dad with a son Ava's age, and he seems like a nice guy."

"He seems like a nice guy?" he repeated. "You only talked to him for a few minutes. He could be an ex-con or a serial killer for all you know."

"You need to stop watching *CSI: Miami*. It's making you suspicious of everyone!"

"I'm not kidding, Jariah. This is serious. There are a lot of sick wackos out there who like to prey on lonely women."

"I'm not lonely." She laughed. "I'm a hopeless romantic. There's a *big* difference."

The sound of her amusement grated on his nerves. Not because it was annoying, but because he didn't appreciate her making light of his warning. "I know what I'm talking about. If you're not careful you could get hurt, or worse, assaulted—"

"That's not going to happen. I teach self-defense classes at Premier Fitness." Squaring her shoulders, she lifted her chin and met his gaze head-on. "Last year, a teenager tried to snatch my purse outside of the mall, and I brought him down so hard he burst into tears!"

Nicco believed her story, but he didn't share her laughter. Spotting the white business card in her hand, he took it from her and inspected it. "'Edison Wayne, Attorney at Law'?" he read, wrinkling his nose. "The guy sounds like a square."

"I'm not looking for Mr. Excitement. I'm looking for an honest, sincere man who loves children and wants to be in a serious, committed relationship."

"You don't want much."

Jariah scoffed and wore a sad face. "Tell that to the guys on my online dating app. Apparently, my standards are too high."

"Online dating is a terrible idea. Do you know how

many psychos troll the internet looking for single, vulnerable women like you?" Nicco recognized that he was shouting, and that his eyelids were twitching manically, but he couldn't control his temper. The thought of Jariah going out with other men—perfect strangers at that—made his blood boil and his head throb.

"I don't need you or anyone else to look out for me. I can take care of myself."

Her cold, terse tone told Nicco he'd struck a nerve; no doubt he'd pissed her off. He'd put his size-twelve foot in his mouth, and would need the Jaws of Life to extract it. But instead of apologizing for hurting her feelings, he said, "I just don't want you putting yourself in harm's way."

"What I do in my spare time and who I go out with is none of your business."

"This isn't your free time," Nicco shot back. He felt a burning sensation in his chest, and didn't know if it was a rush of anger or desire. "In the future, please refrain from picking up men during company time."

Her eyes narrowed with righteous indignation.

Nicco knew he was being unreasonable, and that he had no right to give Jariah a hard time for talking to the attorney, but he couldn't control his feelings—at least not where she was concerned. "Now, if you're finished flirting with everyone inside the lobby, I'd like to go. I have a schedule to keep."

Without another word, Nicco took Jariah by the arm and led her through the sliding glass doors. Outside, he opened the passenger door of his Lamborghini parked at the curb, and watched as Jariah put on her seat belt. His hands were itching to touch her, to hold her in his arms, but he knew now was not the time to put the moves on her.

The air inside the car was thick, consumed with tension, but Nicco pretended not to notice. Behind the wheel, cruising through downtown Miami, he decided he'd waited long enough. He had to tell Jariah the truth before some slick-talking clown stole her away.

Nicco glanced at her, and almost lost control of the car when she crossed her legs. His testosterone level spiked, and his erection grew inside his boxer briefs. Jariah was the kind of woman men fantasized about making love to, and Nicco was no different. He wanted her more than he'd ever wanted anyone before. There was a toughness about her that he found incredibly sexy—even when they argued, and got on each other's nerves. That's why he was going to lay all his cards on the table and hope to God that Jariah didn't laugh in his face.

Chapter 11

The Wine Cellar, a by-appointment-only wine boutique, was known for its swank location, esteemed clientele, and ridiculously expensive liquor. And when Jariah entered the store and saw the Vincent van Gogh paintings, the cushy furniture and the cutting-edge decor she understood why. An elegant establishment, rich in style, substance and class, it was no surprise that the staff was comprised of young, attractive blondes, or that all of the patrons were dripping in bling.

Bottles were on display library-style, and the vaulted ceilings and brass chandeliers gave the wine boutique a cathedral feel. Classical music was playing, and the air smelled like pastries. The low, muted lights were relaxing—which was exactly what Jariah needed. She was angry that Nicco had snapped at her back at the office, and had no intention of speaking to him during the appointment. Hell, if he could be immature, so could she.

"Welcome to The Wine Cellar, Mr. Morretti. We're so glad to have you here with us again." A female wine steward dressed in a slinky red dress appeared, wearing a smile that showcased every tooth. "I've set you up in one of our private tasting rooms at the rear of the boutique."

"Thank you, Christi. Please lead the way."

"Yes, of course. It would be my pleasure." The wide-eyed steward was so busy gazing at Nicco, she backed into a wine barrel and stumbled. Righting herself, she regained her composure and spun on her heels. "I selected some exquisite brands for you to sample…"

"Are you coming?"

Nicco offered his hand, but Jariah stepped past him and followed the loquacious steward through the boutique. He was her boss, not her father, and she wasn't putting up with any of his macho, tough-guy crap today. The man had a serious attitude problem, and an ego that could rival a rap star, and if he thought he could push her around he was sadly mistaken.

Much like the rest of the boutique, the private tasting room was decked out in dark, gleaming wood. Leather-bound books and magazines covered the end tables, plush chairs were situated around the room, and flat-screen TVs were mounted on the sable-brown walls. Bread baskets, wine bottles, miniature glasses and silver trays overflowing with hors d'oeuvres covered the table.

"Mr. Morretti, please feel free to peruse our vast collection of wines," the steward said, gesturing to the shelves behind her. "With more than a hundred samples to enjoy, I'm confident you'll find that perfect gem to add to your restaurant's menu."

"I'm ready to get started. How about you?" Nicco picked up one of the trays and swept his free hand across it with more flair than a British butler. "The stuffed mushrooms taste amazing with full-bodied wines, and…"

Jariah's stomach rumbled in hungry anticipation. *It wouldn't hurt to sample one or two, would it?* She was still mad at Nicco for insulting her, but she took a healthy bite of the stuffed mushroom. It tasted delicious, moist and flavorful, and within seconds she had devoured three.

"Try the baked brie," he encouraged. "It's one of my personal favorites."

Happy to oblige, she sampled the appetizer. "I better stop or I'll split my dress!"

Laughing, they stood side-by-side, reading the information cards for each wine sample.

"Let's just jump right in. It's more fun that way." Winking lasciviously, Nicco picked up two miniature glasses and handed one to Jariah. "*Per un rapporto di lunga e prospera.* Cheers!"

To a long and prosperous relationship? His toast threw her, made her wonder exactly what he was referring to, but she dismissed the thought from her mind. Of course he was talking about work. She was his assistant, and it didn't matter that she secretly lusted after him.

As they tasted the wine samples, Nicco questioned her about the flavors and brands she liked the best, and even fed her caviar. Enjoying herself immensely, she listened to the female steward relay relevant information about each brand and vineyard.

"We need a moment to discuss in private," Nicco announced.

"Of course, no problem, I'll get out of your hair." Christi hustled around the table, snatching up the empty food trays. "If you need anything, just press zero on the phone and I'll be back before you can say Cabernet Sauvignon!"

The steward left and closed the door behind her.

"Are you still mad at me?"

Nicco's question caught Jariah off guard, but instead of lying to make him feel better about acting like a jerk, she told him the truth. "I didn't appreciate what you said, but I'm not the kind of person to hold a grudge. I can move past it, but the next time you disrespect me you'll be looking for *another* executive assistant."

"Don't hold back. Tell me how you really feel," Nicco joked, returning his empty glass to the table. His attempt to lighten the mood earned him a frosty glare. Undeterred, he moved closer until they were face-to-face. "Do you feel better now that you've given me hell?"

"Yes, as a matter of fact, I do."

His gaze held her hostage, refused to let her go.

"You're like a steel magnolia. Soft on the outside, and hard as metal on the inside."

"I don't know if I should be flattered or offended."

"You're not just any girl, Jariah, you're special and I hate the idea of you hooking up with guys online. If you want to go to a show, or a movie or out for dinner, I'm your man."

"You're not my man, Nicco. You're my boss."

"I love when we're together," he confessed, brushing his knuckles against her cheek. "You make me feel things I've never felt before."

"I—I—I do," she stammered, taken aback by his confession.

"Yes, you do."

Jariah stopped breathing. Her hands were shaking hard and fast, and she was so nervous she couldn't stand still. *This can't be happening. I must be dreaming.*

"When you're around I can't think straight." He sounded conflicted, as if he was struggling with a moral dilemma. "I think about you all the time, and when we're apart I wonder what you're doing and if by some stroke of good luck you're thinking about me, too."

Her internal alarm blared inside her head. Nicco was playing mind games with her—just like Mrs. Reddick said he would—and his pitiful attempt to lure her into bed was sickening. Disgust must have clouded her face because he cupped her chin and forced her to meet his gaze. "I'm not bullshitting you. I'm for real."

"No, you're not. You're a player who gets off on screwing your staff," she shot back, determined to speak her mind. "How many of your subordinates have you slept with over the years? Five? Ten? Twenty?"

His face fell, and his eyes darkened with contempt.

Guilt troubled her conscience. She'd gone too far, said too much, and when Nicco dropped his head and raked a hand through his dark, lush hair, Jariah wished she had bitten her tongue. "You have a reputation, and—"

"I know, but instead of believing the hype, why not get to know me for yourself and form your own opinion? I haven't been a Boy Scout, but I'm not the man whore people make me out to be on social media."

He took another step closer and lowered his hands from her cheek to her waist. Swallowing hard, Jariah pretended she wasn't affected by his touch, but she was—in every way—and her aching breasts and moist clit proved just how much she desired him.

Something Mrs. Reddick said weeks earlier came back to her. "What happened to your previous assistant?" she asked. "Why is she no longer working for you?"

"She found a better gig, I guess."

Jariah heard Nicco's cell phone ring, and welcomed the interruption. Their conversation was getting heated, and she needed a moment to clear her head. She expected Nicco to slip out of the room to take the call, but he didn't. Instead, he took out his iPhone, switched it off and placed it on the table. "Now, where were we?"

"*We* weren't anywhere." Jariah pressed herself flat against the wall and propped a hand on her hip to prove she meant business. It didn't matter that she yearned for his kiss, or that her body was on fire—they could never be lovers, and nothing he said or did would ever change that. "I won't sleep with you. Not today, not tomorrow, not next week."

"That's not what I'm about. This isn't about sex or about me trying to play you, either. This is about me wanting to spend time with you after hours, *outside* of the office."

His words gave her pause.

"Mi sono rettilinei. Voglio a corte, Jariah."

"Court me?" she repeated, amused by his words and the boyish expression on his face. "What is this? The Elizabethan era?"

Nicco chuckled. "I want to get to know you better and I think going out on dates a few nights a week is definitely the way to go, don't you?"

He flashed a broad grin, one that made Jariah's heart flutter and dance. Fidgeting with her hands, she dropped her gaze to the plush beige carpet. Not because she was embarrassed, but because she didn't want Nicco to read her like a book. She wanted to get to know him better, too, behind closed doors, and feared he'd take one look at her and see the truth in her eyes.

"No one has to know we're seeing each other. It'll be our little secret…"

Fear and excitement filled her. Their conversation was getting more outrageous by the second, but damn it, if flirting with him wasn't turning her on. *Why does the thought of sneaking around with Nicco excite me?* Jariah wondered, confused by her feelings. *What is it about him that makes me nervous and giddy at the same time?*

"Let's do dinner and a movie tomorrow night," he proposed. "I know you have to drop Ava off at her grandparent's house, so I'm cool with meeting you at the theater."

"Aren't your brothers flying in tonight?"

"No, they'll be here tomorrow night. If you're not busy, I'd love if you could join us for dinner," he said. "They're going to love you, I just know it."

Jariah's body was humming with excitement at the prospect of going on an honest-to-goodness date with Nicco, but she played it cool and pretended as if she wasn't completely sold on the idea. "I'll think about it and get back to you."

"What's there to think about? I'm not inviting you to Vegas for a weekend of booze and debauchery, I'm inviting you to dinner and a movie."

Laughter fell from Jariah's lips. "The last time we made plans to meet *you* were late, so forgive me for being leery about taking you up on your offer."

Nicco wore an innocent face. "You must have me confused with someone else, because only an ass would make a beautiful woman like you wait."

"I wholeheartedly agree!"

"Mi piace il tuo intelligente, bocca fresca, e che splendido corpo di vostro."

You think I'm hot? Seriously? No way! But I'm a size eight, not a size two and you have a thing for thin women with big, fake boobs!

"I'll be at Paragon Theaters at six o'clock sharp, and if I'm late I'll owe you a massage."

His breath tickled her ear, and when he trailed a finger down the length of her cheek, Jariah swallowed a gasp. His touch made her wet and desperate for more.

"Would you like that?" he asked, leaning into her, his smoldering gaze probing and intense. "Would you like to feel my hands all over your body?"

You have no idea.

Electricity crackled between them, causing the air in the room to swelter. Nicco seized Jariah around the waist and drew her right up to his chest. Then, the unthinkable happened—he kissed her. He brushed his lips against her mouth, gently at first, but the kiss quickly evolved into a passionate, desperate plea. Nicco kissed her with urgency, with a passionate, ferocious heat.

They'd crossed the line, jumped headfirst over it, and now there was no turning back.

Burying her hands in his hair, Jariah grabbed a fistful of curls and stirred her fingers around his dark, lush locks. Playing in his hair increased her sexual hunger. Finally, after weeks of stolen glances and lascivious smiles, she knew just how delicious his mouth tasted. And it was better than she'd imagined. Beyond her wildest dreams. His lips were flavored with wine, carried a hint of spice, and the intoxicating blend made her delirious with need.

For a split second, Jariah considered fleeing the private tasting room, but she was helpless to resist his kiss, and his sweet, sensuous caress. Her ear throbbed. Tremors erupted inside her body, and she could feel the blood rushing to her tingling sex.

Devouring his lips, she inclined her head toward him and boldly gave him everything she had. A wild, primal hunger took over her body. Hot with lust, she locked her arms around his neck and pressed herself flat against his solid, toned physique.

Standing chest-to-chest, their lips, mouths and hands greedily explored each other's flesh. The kiss was long overdue, and not only well worth the wait, but the best thing Jariah had ever experienced. His lips were pure ecstasy, and more addictive than Godiva chocolate. She felt alive, energized, and the more they kissed and stroked each other, the harder it was to keep her head. Her lust veered out of control, had her saying and doing things out of character. Nicco was the world's greatest kisser, a pro when it came to pleasing a woman with his lips, and Jariah craved him in ways he couldn't imagine.

"You knew from day one this was bound to happen, right?" His voice was a husky growl, but he stroked her cheeks with loving tenderness. "From the moment we met, I knew it was just a matter of time before we surrendered to our desires."

The truth got stuck in her throat. Yes, deep down, Jariah always knew this day would come but she never imagined it would be so soon. Her mind and her body were in turmoil, and the cravings of her flesh warred against her morals.

"I want you so bad it hurts," Nicco groaned, between each passionate kiss. "I want to rip off your dress, bend you over the table and love you until I'm spent."

At the thought, a fierce, powerful contraction erupted between Jariah's legs. She should have been offended, appalled by his crude, raunchy talk, but she was so turned on by his words her body was a raging inferno. Every breath was a fight. In public, Nicco played the role of the wounded, misunderstood bad-boy to the hilt, but behind closed doors he bore a different persona. He had a softer, gentler side, one she was wholly attracted to, and Jariah couldn't imagine anything better than making sweet love to him.

The more she rubbed herself against him, the more urgent his kiss. They were connected, finally experiencing the joy of each other's mouths, hands and bodies. She felt wanton, naughty, and couldn't rein in her hot, weak flesh.

Caught up, Jariah couldn't bring herself to stop kissing him, to quit rubbing her full, aching breasts against his chest. His touch was out of this world, like no other. Jariah felt a hint of his tongue, just the tip, and all but lost her mind. She clung to him desperately, held him tight.

"From the moment I saw you, I knew you were 'the one.'" Nicco took her hand and placed it over his heart. "I felt it in here, deep in my soul, and over the past few weeks my feelings for you have only gotten stronger. You're all I think about, Jariah, and every night when I close my eyes I see your beautiful face."

Stunned, Jariah felt her mouth gape open. His confession and the strength of his gaze blew her away. There was no way, after working together for a month that his feelings could be so deep, so intense. He was playing. Had to be.

Why is it so shocking? her conscience asked. *You feel the same way and the only reason you're not sexing him on the couch is because your unmentionables don't match!*

"I'll never, ever do anything to hurt you, Jariah. You have my word."

Jariah didn't speak, couldn't vocalize her feelings. His words penetrated the thick walls around her heart, and the kiss he dropped on her lips brought a girlish smile to her mouth. Her throat was dry, her legs were shaking something fierce and her sex was throbbing so hard she ached to feel him deep inside her.

Pulling herself together, she surfaced from her sexual miasma and pushed all thoughts of making love to Nicco out of her mind. "We're getting way ahead of ourselves," she said, determined to be the voice of reason. "It was just a kiss. It didn't mean anything."

"You're wrong. It meant everything to me."

Me, too, but I'm terrified you're going to hurt me.

Taking her hands in his, he tenderly kissed each palm.

"Nicco, you're a great guy, but—"

Wincing as if in physical pain, he pressed a finger to her mouth, and nodded solemnly. "I know. You don't have to say it. If someone found out about us it would ruin your reputation."

"That's not it," Jariah said, smiling sadly. "I'm a single mom."

A frown marred his features. "What does that have to do with anything?"

"Isn't it obvious? Ava and I are a package deal, and that will never change."

"I know, and that's a plus, not a minus."

"Nicco, I'm not interested in having an office romance or a tawdry summer fling. I want to get married and have more children."

His smile was pure sin. "Sounds good to me. Want to start practicing right now?"

"I'm serious," she said, struggling to keep a straight face.

"So, am I."

"You're ready to be in a committed relationship?"

"Three months ago, I couldn't fathom settling down, but since meeting you, it's all I can think about. Crazy, huh?"

"Insane," she breathed, her head spinning faster than the ceiling fan above them.

"Think you could get used to me being around 24/7?"

Are you kidding? In a heartbeat! But instead of speaking her mind, she asked the most logical question. "What now, Nicco? Where do we go from here?"

"We're going to kiss and make out some more." Nicco dropped his gaze to her cleavage and slowly licked his lips. "Is that okay with you?"

Jariah heard the word, "Absolutely," fall from her lips, and raised her mouth to meet his kiss. As they came together, a young, breathy voice filled the air.

"I'm sorry to bother you, but I've been knocking on the door with no success."

Over his shoulder, Jariah peeped at the female steward, standing inside the doorway. Her face gave nothing away, but she sensed the woman's displeasure.

Despite the pep talk, Jariah felt a stab of guilt and was embarrassed about getting caught fooling around with Nicco. She tried to move out of his arms, but he tightened his hold around her waist and gave her a peck on the lips.

"What is it?" he asked, tossing a glance over his shoulder at the steward. "I'm in the middle of something."

"I know, sir, and I apologize for the interruption, but you have a phone call."

"Take a message."

"I think this is a call you'll want to take," the steward said. "Someone's been shot."

Chapter 12

"Shot!" The word exploded like a bullet out of Nicco's mouth. He snatched the phone out of the steward's hand, put it to his ear and stalked over to the window. Curious and concerned, Jariah stared at Nicco, hoping that everything would be all right. She knew from past conversations that he was a proud mama's boy, ridiculously close to his brothers Demetri and Rafael, and that he was concerned about the break-in at Dolce Vita. Had there now been a shooting at the restaurant? Was someone he loved fatally hurt?

Hearing a noise behind her, Jariah glanced over her shoulder. The steward cut her eyes, and pursed her lips in disdain. Tossing her hair over her shoulders, she turned and stomped out of the room.

What was that *all about?* Jariah stared down at her clothes, realizing her boobs were on display, lace push-up bra and all, and cringed. By now, the entire store would know she'd made out with Nicco, and that made her feel cheap, dirty. *I should have exercised more self-control.*

More? Her conscience mocked. *When it comes to, Nicco, you have no self-control!*

A sudden thought occurred to her, increasing her anxiety. Was this a setup? Had Nicco brought her to the wine boutique to help him select wines or to put the moves on her? His words flooded her mind.

You knew from day one this was bound to happen, right? From the moment we met, I knew it was just a matter of time before we surrendered to our desires.

Jariah knew then without a doubt that Nicco had planned this little jaunt to the wine boutique for one reason and one reason only: to put the moves on her. Feelings of guilt and shame engulfed her, and her head throbbed in pain. Was Mrs. Reddick right? Was getting her into bed nothing more than a game to him? One she would inevitably lose?

"Son of a bitch! How could you be so stupid?"

Nicco's harsh, biting tone made Jariah flinch. Pacing the room like a caged animal, he yelled into the phone with such ferocity the windows shook.

"Gerald, don't give me that crap. I pay you very well to ensure things like this don't happen," he roared. "Was Mr. Sarmento badly injured?"

Listening to Nicco berate the head of his security division was not only upsetting, it was infuriating. The ex-navy SEAL was a quiet, soft-spoken man with a genial demeanor. Available day and night, he worked tirelessly for Morretti Incorporated and seemed to genuinely love his job.

"Meet me back at the office in an hour. We'll drive to Jackson Memorial together."

Nicco ended the call. "Grab your things. We have to go."

Quickly, Jariah retrieved her purse. "What's going on?"

"It's a long story. I'll tell you in the car."

At the entrance of the boutique, Nicco apologized to the owner for his hasty departure and promised to return next week to place his order.

Inside the car, as they sped up the block, Nicco explained what happened that morning when his security team and the Portuguese businessman were leaving the Beach Bentley Hotel.

"An armed gunman surprised them as they were boarding the private elevator, and during the scuffle, Mr. Sarmento was shot."

"Oh, my goodness, that's terrible. Is Gerald okay? Did he get hurt?"

"Who the hell cares?" Nicco spat, his eyes blazing with fire. "If Gerald had done his job, Mr. Sarmento wouldn't be lying in a hospital bed with a gunshot wound to the chest. I have half a mind to fire him, and the two idiots working with him, too."

"Nicco, you're being unreasonable. You don't even know what happened."

"I never asked your opinion."

Instead of lashing back, Jariah crossed her arms and stared out the windshield.

"Stay out of this," Nicco warned, his voice a harsh, grating tone. Stepping on the gas, he shot onto the freeway and switched lanes with the skill of a championship-winning race-car driver. "Gerald's a big boy. He can take it."

"That still doesn't make it right. He's dealing with a lot right now and you're—"

"How the hell do *you* know? Do you have the hots for the guy? Is that why you're sticking up for him?" Jaw clenched and nostrils flaring, he tightened his grip on the steering wheel. "Just so you know, Gerald's married, and his wife is pregnant."

"I know. She was hospitalized last week, and he's worried sick."

"What?" Nicco shot her a puzzled look. "Who told you that?"

"No one. I overheard him talking to Mrs. Reddick in the staff room a couple days ago."

"Why didn't you tell me?"

"Because it's none of my business," Jariah said, suddenly feeling like a hypocrite.

Exhaling a deep breath, Nicco sank back in his seat. They drove in silence for several minutes, and when he finally spoke, his voice was hollow and his eyes were filled with regret. "I had no idea Gerald's wife was in the hospital. Now I feel like an ass for going off on him."

As you should, she thought, but wisely held her tongue. Making Nicco feel worse than he already did wasn't going to help matters. To lighten the mood, she said, "Don't worry. There'll be plenty of time for you to apologize to Gerald later."

"Why do I have a feeling you're going to hold me to that?" he asked, raising a brow.

"Because if you don't, I'll tell your brothers you play 'Dance Dance Revolution' on your Wii!"

"I know you're in a rush to pick up Ava from day camp, but if it's not too much trouble can you cancel all of my afternoon meetings before you take off?" Nicco asked, marching briskly through the reception area. "I'd do it myself, but I'm anxious to get to the hospital."

"Don't worry. I'll handle it," Jariah promised.

"And make sure you speak directly to Claudia Jeffries-Medina. Tell her there's been an emergency and that I'm sorry for canceling at the last minute."

"Will do, and to be on the safe side, I'll also notify your contacts by email."

"Thanks, babe, I really appreciate it."

"Nicco, don't call me that," she hissed. "Not here."

He wore an amused face. "You know I own the company, right?"

"Nothing's changed. I'm still your employee and you're still my boss."

"And?"

"And when we're at the office it's business as usual."

Nicco grabbed her around the waist and kissed her cheek. "That sounds boring."

"It wouldn't look good if a potential client or staff member walked in and saw us like this," Jariah said, breaking free of his grasp and smoothing a hand over her dress. The tenth floor was deserted, but she glanced around, convinced Mrs. Reddick was going to burst out of the washroom, screaming at her. "Let's get down to work. Gerald's going to be here any minute, and I don't want him to catch us slacking off."

Chuckling, Nicco pushed open his office door and strode inside.

"I've been a *really* bad girl this week, and I want you to spank me."

Frowning, Jariah peered over Nicco's shoulder in search of the female with the sultry voice. A half-naked beauty was sitting on the middle of his desk, holding a black leather paddle, purring like a Siamese kitten. She had silky hair, hot pink lips and a body that could tempt a man of the cloth. Jariah stared at the light-skinned temptress, stunned by the woman's audacity. *Doesn't she see me standing here? Isn't she embarrassed about me—a perfect stranger—seeing her in her bra and G-string?*

"Estelle, what are you doing here?" Nicco asked. "You're supposed to be in St. Lucia."

"I know how much you love surprises, so after my *Penthouse* shoot wrapped up, I decided to come pay you a visit." The woman spoke with a heavy Caribbean accent, and crossed her legs with more flair than an exotic dancer. "Do you like my new paddle?"

Licking her lips, she leaped off the desk and sashayed

provocatively across the room. "I'm anxious to try it out, so get rid of that girl and let's get down and dirty…"

Jariah swiveled her neck and propped a hand on her waist.

"Get going." The woman flapped her hands in the air as if she was swatting a pesky fly. "You're messing up our groove."

Her dismissal was like a slap in the face.

"Are you hard of hearing or just stupid?"

"Estelle, don't talk to my girl like that."

"Your girl?" Raising her eyebrows sky-high, she wrinkled her nose. "You're kidding, right?"

Shame and embarrassment burned Jariah's skin. Despite standing eye-to-eye with the leggy model, she couldn't help feeling small and insignificant. Trembling, her eyes burning with tears, she turned and fled the office.

"Jariah, don't go! I can explain. It's not as bad as it looks.…"

You're right, Nicco. It's worse!

As Jariah rushed through the reception area, she heard the elevator ping. The doors slid open, and Gerald stepped off, looking haggard and spent. "Hello, Ms. Brooks."

Too choked up to speak, Jariah hurled herself inside the small metal box and frantically jabbed the down button. The doors closed, sealing her inside the elevator with her hurt and frustration. She was angry at herself for running out of Nicco's office like a scared little girl, and furious at Nicco for trying to play her like a fool.

Slumping against the wall, she closed her eyes and dropped her face in her hands. Fighting back tears, she inwardly chastised herself for the way she'd acted back at the wine boutique. *How could I have been so foolish? How could I actually believe that Nicco could be interested in me when he has* Penthouse *models throwing themselves at him? And why in the world did I let him kiss me?*

Her cell phone rang from inside her purse. Jariah decided to let her voice mail take the call then remembered she was still technically on the clock and whipped her BlackBerry out of her purse.

The phone had stopped ringing, but started up again seconds later.

"Yes?" she snapped, reluctantly putting her cell to her ear. "What do you want?"

"Come back. I got rid of her."

"Was that before or *after* you broke in her new paddle?"

"Jariah, I haven't looked at another woman since the day we met."

"Right," she said sourly.

"Estelle's gone, and she's not coming back."

"How long have you guys been lovers?"

Nicco paused, and then released a heavy sigh. "It's not important."

"It is to me."

"We used to hook up whenever she came to town, but now we're over. I told her that you're my girl, and she left."

"Just like that."

"Just like that. Please come back. We need to talk."

He couldn't see her, but she shook her head, refusing to entertain the idea. "You have to go to Jackson Memorial, and I have calls to make," she said, checking the time on her watch. "If it's okay with you, I'll work from home for the rest of the day."

Silence descended on the line.

"Hello? Nicco? Are you still there?"

"Yeah, I'm here."

"Did you hear what I said?"

"Yes, but I really wish you'd come back so we can talk about us."

There is no us. "Nicco, I'm fine."

"That you are," he said smoothly, his voice regaining

its warmth, its cheer. "Fine, I'll cool my heels for now, but tomorrow you're mine, all mine, no excuses."

Jariah wanted to argue, but she didn't have the energy. She was emotionally spent, so drained she had no fight left in her. It was all too much—Nicco's heartfelt confession, the kiss, his old flame popping up in his office—and the only place Jariah wanted to be tomorrow night was at home in bed. She'd had enough excitement today to last her a lifetime, and decided instead of beating around the bush, to be straight-up with Nicco. "I don't think we should date. It's a bad idea, and there could be serious repercussions for both of us."

"I'm sorry about what just went down, but nothing's changed. I still want to spend time with you this weekend, and I won't let you blow me off."

"I have to go. I, ah, have another call coming through, and it could be Ava. Bye."

Click. Nicco dropped the phone back in the cradle and slumped in his chair, thinking about the mess he'd gotten himself into. He only had himself to blame—he should have cut ties with Estelle weeks ago. If he had, he wouldn't be beating himself up now.

Why hadn't Estelle just stayed in St. Lucia? Why did she have to show up today of all days? Finally, after weeks of sweating Jariah, she was opening up to him, even letting her guard down, but in the space of an hour, all of his hard work had gone up in smoke. Now her wall was back up, firmly erected around her heart, and that sucked, because he had plans for her. Big plans that would prove how much he cared for her.

Needing something to calm his nerves, Nicco opened his bottom drawer in search of his Cuban cigars. He reached for the yellow box bearing the Romeo Y Julieta logo, but he quickly remembered his promise to Jariah and slammed the drawer shut. He hadn't had a cigar in weeks but he refused to go back on his word. He didn't want to disappoint her. Not now. Not when they were on the verge of something special.

Shaking his head, he wore a rueful smile. His parents were going to love Jariah and not just because she was a spirited young woman who freely spoke her mind. She'd succeeded in getting him to quit smoking, and once his mom found out, she'd probably propose to Jariah on his behalf. The thought should have terrified Nicco, but it didn't. In fact, the idea of sleeping with Jariah nestled in his arms every night filled his heart with joy.

"I'm here, boss. Sorry it took me so long. Traffic was crazy on the 1-95."

Gerald stood in the doorway, his expression grim. Nicco wondered if the ex-navy SEAL looked pitiful because he felt guilty about what happened at the Beach Bentley Hotel, or because he was worried about his pregnant wife. Nicco remembered what Jariah had said in the car, and knew, deep down, that she was right—he shouldn't have berated Gerald—but he couldn't bring himself to apologize. Later, when Mr. Sarmento was discharged from the hospital and the police found the crook behind the brazen early-morning attack, he'd make things right with Gerald. And Jariah, too, because after the drama Estelle had just caused he owed her big-time.

Up on his feet, he pushed back his chair and scooped up his car keys. Thoughts of Jariah filled his mind as he drove to Jackson Memorial Hospital. Smoothing things over with Gerald would be easy, but Nicco suspected it was going to take a hell of a lot more than a steak entrée and a round of beers to convince Jariah to give him another chance.

Chapter 13

Teeming with mansions and luxury vehicles with personalized license plates, Coconut Grove had long been home to Miami's richest, most esteemed residents. But no couple was more revered than Lee and Stella Covington. The plastic surgeon and his socialite wife proudly flaunted their wealth and routinely entertained celebrities and politicians in their mansion. "We're here." Jariah drove through the wrought-iron gates and parked in front of the bronze Zeus fountain. She turned around to remind Ava to be on her best behavior, but before she could get a word out, her daughter threw open the back door and took off running up the driveway. "Ava Faith Covington, get back here."

"Bye, Mom!" she yelled, with a quick wave over her shoulder. "I love you!"

By the time Jariah grabbed her daughter's overnight bag and made the trek up the winding cobblestone walkway, Ms. Covington was standing on her doorstep.

"Hello, Stella. How are you?

"Ava, why don't you go around back and say hello to Grandpa Lee?" Mrs. Covington kissed her granddaughter on the top of her head, then steered her toward the backyard. "He is playing with the poodles, but if you ask nicely he might take you for a ride on his golf cart."

"Yippee!" Ava cheered. "Maybe he'll even let me drive."

Before she could take off again, Jariah gave her daughter a hug. "Call me before you go to bed, and be a good girl for Grandma and Grandpa."

"Don't worry, Mom, I will. See you on Sunday!"

Once Ava left, the smile slid off Mrs. Covington's face. "Do you *have* to buy my granddaughter bargain basement clothes?" she asked, folding her long, bony arms across her chest. "A couple washes and that pink Dora dress will be a tattered, frizzy mess."

"There's nothing wrong with the clothes at. J. C. Penney. They're cute and affordable."

"And cheap."

"It doesn't make sense buying expensive designer outfits for Ava when she's just going to ruin them playing outside with her friends."

"It's no wonder! What do you expect when you shop at thrift stores?"

"The clothes at Target are every bit as good as the clothes in Nordstrom."

"And I suppose you think Jack in the Box is a fine dining establishment," she scoffed. "But you would. You *were* raised in Overtown."

Jariah warned herself to keep a cool head. Every time she did something Mrs. Covington didn't like, she insulted her old neighborhood. Overtown was an impoverished community, overrun with crime, drugs and poverty, but Jariah wouldn't trade her humble beginnings for anything in the world. At a very early age, her parents had taught her the value of self-respect and hard work, and all of the struggles and hardships she'd witnessed in their housing project had made her the woman she was today. And for that reason alone, she refused to take any of Stella Covington's crap. "I'm proud of where I come from."

"Of course you are, dear," she said, her tone dripping with sarcasm. "It must be *very* exciting to see your old neighborhood featured on the evening news every single night."

Her words hit a nerve. Thankfully, Jariah didn't see Mrs. Covington often, because whenever she did, the witch of the south made a point of insulting her. But Jariah wasn't ashamed that she'd been raised in the inner city, or that her parents had factory jobs.

"You should thank your lucky stars you won that scholarship to the University of Miami, or you never would have met my sweet Wesley."

Sweet? Ha! "I didn't win anything," Jariah said, feeling her temperature rise. "I had the highest GPA in my high school, and I worked damn hard to earn that academic scholarship."

"I have to give it to you, Jariah. You're much smarter than you look," Mrs. Covington continued. "You met my son, got knocked up and moved into his apartment all in one semester. If that isn't ingenuity, I don't know what is…"

Jariah wore a blank face, but inside she was on fire. She imagined herself snatching the curly wig off Mrs. Covington's head and flinging it into the infinity pond, but took a deep breath instead. Any other day, she would've fired back with a zinger of her own, but she wasn't trading insults with the crotchety housewife today. She had a two o'clock appointment at Glamour Girlz Salon. If she was late her beautician would give her slot to someone else, and she wanted to look extraspecial for her date with Nicco.

At the thought of him, her frown morphed into a smile. Jariah could hardly wait for six o'clock to roll around. Nicco had called that morning while she was making breakfast, and the moment she heard his voice her spirits soared. They'd talked and laughed for over an hour, but as Jariah listened to Nicco describe the plans he'd made for their date, her fears returned with a vengeance.

"I still think this is a bad idea," she'd said, unable to shake free of her doubts, or images of Mrs. Reddick chasing her around the offices of Morretti Incorporated with a letter opener. "What if we run into someone we know during dinner?"

"You worry too much. Loosen up. We're going to have a great time tonight."

"I'll loosen up as soon as you do."

"Me?" he'd scoffed. "Woman, please, I'm so loose I could teach your hot yoga class!"

Hours later, the joke still made Jariah crack up. Nicco was taking her out tonight, and although she wouldn't admit it to anyone—not even herself—she was looking forward to spending time with him. The kiss they'd shared yesterday at The Wine Cellar was all Jariah could think about, and she was hungry for more—

"Ava is a Covington, and I expect her to look and act like such at all times."

The sound of Stella's loud, shrill voice yanked Jariah out of her reverie. "She's only six years old. You can't expect her to be perfect."

"Yes, I can," she shot back, her self-righteous tone as haughty as ever. "Wesley was a model child, and he never gave me any trouble whatsoever." She paused. "If I wasn't so busy with my charity work, I'd take Ava in and raise her as my own."

Over my dead body.

"Since it's obvious you can't handle, Ava, you should relinquish custody to my son."

"Which son? Do you have another child I don't know about?"

"Wesley is a terrific father, and a noble young man with great morals."

You are so delusional, Jariah thought, rolling her eyes behind the safety of her sunglasses. *Wesley grumbles about paying child support and routinely breaks plans with Ava.*

"It's also obvious that you're still bitter."

"Bitter?" Jariah repeated, incredulous. "I'm the one who called off our engagement."

"That's because deep down you know you're not good enough for my son, and it was killing you inside."

Jariah tossed her head back and laughed out loud. "That was a good one. Thanks, Stella. I really needed that."

"Go ahead, yuck it up, but you will never, *ever* be a Covington!"

I know. Talk about a stroke of good luck! Jariah knew she was adding fuel to the fire, but she couldn't resist saying, "Thank God for that," as she turned and walked back to her car.

"Honey chile, where are you going? You look hella hot!"

Jariah wheeled around, saw Felicia double-parked behind her car and waved. "Hey, girl. What's up? Where are you rushing off to?"

"You first." Displaying a coy smirk on her lips, she leaned out the window of her red SUV. "Don't tell me. You and that fine-ass boss of yours are meeting up at one of those ritzy downtown hotels to get your freak on!"

Ever since Nicco and Richie had come over for dinner last month, Felicia had been questioning her incessantly about their relationship. Her neighbor was convinced they were lovers, and although Jariah fervently denied the accusation, her friend believed otherwise.

"You're hot for that gorgeous Italian millionaire, and he's hot for you. Just admit it."

"No, I'm not," she said, avoiding Felicia's gaze. Jariah

didn't want anyone to know about her plans with Nicco—especially the neighborhood gossip—so she did the only thing she could and she lied. "If you must know, I'm meeting my old college roommate for coffee."

"In that sexy getup? Yous a damn lie!" Her demeanor turned serious, and her tone was filled with concern. "Be careful, Jariah. Your boss has a reputation for being a heartbreaker, and I'd hate for you or Ava to get hurt."

Me, too, Felicia. That's why I'm going to take things slow.

"Men love the thrill of the chase, and rich guys are the biggest dogs of all," she continued, her tone no-nonsense. "I'm not saying Nicco's going to play you, but it would be crazy for you to think you're the only girl he's kicking it with…"

Jariah nodded as if she was listening intently, but she wasn't. Reading bestselling books on relationships had turned her friend into an amateur shrink. And since Jariah didn't have the time to listen to Felicia's unsolicited advice, she changed the subject. "You look great, and I love your new haircut. Where are you going?"

"For coffee with my old college roommate." Felicia winked, slid her sunglasses on and cranked up her car stereo. "See you later, girlfriend. Have fun with boss man!"

Seconds later, Jariah got inside her car and put on her seat belt. She slid the key into the ignition and turned the lock, but it didn't start. It didn't even make its usual noises. Sweat trickled down her forehead, and the car sweltered with heat, but she continued furiously pumping the gas. Jariah didn't know how long she sat there, willing her temperamental Dodge to start, and when her cell phone rang from deep inside her purse she ignored it.

It rang incessantly, until Jariah couldn't take it anymore. Taking her cell out of her purse, she saw that it was six forty-five, and that she had four missed calls from

Nicco. *No wonder he's blowing up my phone. He thinks I stood him up!*

Taking a deep breath, she put the phone to her ear. "Hello."

"Is everything okay? I've been worried sick about you."

Jariah felt a swell of emotion inside her chest. His voice was filled with concern. Jariah didn't know if it was the heat finally getting to her, or how sweet he sounded, but she fell apart. Her eyes welled up with water, and tears gushed down her cheeks. "I'm still at home. My stupid car won't start."

"Sit tight. I'm on my way."

"Nicco, I'll be fine. I can handle it." Embarrassed that she'd lost her composure, Jariah grabbed a Kleenex from her purse and wiped her face. "I'll just call a tow truck."

"Go inside and relax. I'll take care of everything."

"Are you sure? I feel terrible for inconveniencing you."

"It's no inconvenience at all, and like I told you this morning, nothing is more important to me than seeing you. Now get off the phone and go inside," he ordered.

Twenty minutes later, Jariah spotted a sleek black Jaguar turn in to her complex and knew that Nicco was behind the wheel. He collected luxury vehicles the way most women collected shoes, and drove a different car every day of the week.

Stepping out onto the porch, Jariah waved and walked down the steps. She wanted to run—straight into Nicco's arms—but cautioned herself to not to act like a forlorn teen. But seeing him looking all kinds of sexy in his all-black attire made her heart soar. Diamond earrings twinkled in each ear, and tattoos covered his left arm.

"Hey, you." Nicco hugged her, and every muscle in her body tensed. "What's the matter? Are you still upset because your car died? I told you it's no big deal. It happens."

"That's not it." Jariah glanced nervously around the complex. "Someone could see us."

"And?" he challenged. "You're my lady, and I don't care who knows."

Jariah felt like jumping up and down, but remembered she was a grown woman, not a toddler, and told herself to relax. Inside, Jariah was dancing, but on the surface she played it cool. They weren't a couple, and although she loved the idea of dating Nicco, she knew their attraction wasn't enough to forge a long-term relationship. "I'm not your girl—"

"Not yet, but you will be. Mark my words."

"My, my, aren't we overconfident."

"Not overconfident. Determined."

He stroked her neck softly, nuzzling his chin against her cheek.

"I don't stop until I get what I want," he confessed, his gaze as strong as the sun's blinding rays. "I'm going to make you mine. Just wait and see."

Be still, heart! she warned, aroused by his bold declaration.

Suddenly a loud rumbling noise polluted the air. A blue tow truck was chugging up the block, blaring rock music. Mechanic Motors was embossed on the hood of the truck, and the bearded driver nodded in greeting as he pulled up behind her Dodge.

"Leave everything to me." Nicco took Jariah's car keys out of her hand and dropped a kiss on her cheek. "Wait here. I'll be right back."

Nicco jogged over to the tow truck and spoke to the driver. Seconds later, he was back at Jariah's side, hustling her around the front of his Jaguar.

"Shouldn't we wait for the tow truck driver to remove my car?"

"There's no need. Luciano's a pro. He's got this."

"Do you think he'll have a chance to look at my Dodge tonight?" Jariah asked. "I have to pick up Ava from her grandparents' house on Sunday afternoon, and taking a cab to Coconut Grove would cost me an arm and a leg."

"I'll take you."

"I can't let you do that."

"I want to." Closing the space between them, he cupped her chin in his hands and forced her eyes to meet his. "I want to help, so let me."

His words filled her heart with joy, and the urge to kiss him was so overwhelming she couldn't think straight. Common sense kicked in, but her need for the Italian heart-throb still remained. "I appreciate the offer, but trust me, you do not want to meet Ava's grandmother. She'd take one look at your tattoos and diamond earrings and go into attack mode."

"I guess you haven't noticed, but I have a way with the ladies."

"Not this one," Jariah quipped. "She's so mean she could scare the devil!"

Chapter 14

Dinner was an indulgent, five-course meal at the most expensive restaurant in town. By the time Nicco escorted Jariah out of The Greek Isles, the sun was making its descent, and the sky was bathed in a brilliant yellow-orange hue. Laughter and boisterous conversation carried on the summer breeze, decorative lamps showered the streets with light and a Hispanic teenager dressed in army fatigues recited poetry with the conviction of a Civil Rights Leader.

"What did you think of The Greek Isles?"

"Isn't it obvious? I finished my entrée *and* yours!" Jariah said with a laugh. "The service was outstanding, and you were right about the honey lemon cake. It *was* to die for."

"I hate to say I told you so, but well, I did!"

Nicco chuckled, and the hearty, good-natured sound brought a smile to Jariah's lips.

"Tell me more about Italy," she said, curious to know more about his native country. During dinner, he'd talked much about his relatives in Venice, and the five-room villa he owned in his beloved hometown. "Do you go there every summer?"

"Of course. Sometimes three of four times a year if my schedule permits. My family didn't immigrate to the States until I was twelve, so in my heart Italy will always be home."

"I've always wanted to go, but I've never been. What's it like?"

"Loud, energetic and very much like New York City. There's always something to see and do, and Italians are the most gregarious people in the world. They love to entertain and socialize and nothing matters more to them than their family. Sunday dinners at my grandmother's house were always non-negotiable," he said, his eyes bright and his tone warm.

"I've always dreamed of seeing the Colosseum and Vatican City."

"Then I'll take you. Let's go for New Year's, because no one knows how to party like my Uncle Guido. And he's seventy-five!"

"My ex would never agree to keep Ava."

"He doesn't need to. We'll take her with us."

His voice was firm and final, as if the matter was decided. Shock prevented Jariah from speaking, and her heart was beating so loud she couldn't hear herself think. *Is he for real? Is it possible he cares for me and my daughter or is he just saying what he thinks I want to hear?*

"I'm having a great time with you, Jariah. I only wish we had done this sooner."

Nicco took her hand in his, held it tight, causing her to feel mushy inside. She couldn't remember ever having this much fun on a first date, and wasn't ready for the night to end. There didn't seem to be anything the restaurateur didn't know, and every day he taught her something new. Yesterday, it was how to select the perfect wine, and tonight it was how to order her entrée in Greek. It was awesome being alone with Nicco, laughing, joking and flirting.

Jariah wondered what else the Italian-born businessman had up his sleeve.

As they strolled down Grand Avenue, hand-in-hand, they discussed his brothers' upcoming visit to Miami, and his parents' anniversary bash on Labor Day weekend.

"How did your parents meet?" Jariah asked.

"At Mardi Gras. They spent the weekend together, and when my dad returned to Italy, he sent mom a ticket to come visit. They've been inseparable ever since."

Awed, Jariah shook her head. "Wow, that's some story."

"Pops said it was love at first sight, and the moment I saw you, I knew how he felt."

He angled his head toward her, as if he was going to kiss her, but didn't. Jariah felt a twinge of disappointment. Tonight was about getting to know Nicco better, not jumping his bones.

"What color is your dress?"

"My dress?" Jariah repeated, puzzled. "For what?"

"My parents' anniversary bash of course."

"I'm not going."

Nicco slowed his pace. "Why not? All Morretti Incorporated employees are invited."

"I know, but I haven't been with the company long, and I don't know a lot of people."

And I can't handle Mrs. Reddick giving me the evil eye all night!

"You have to come," he said, grasping her hand tighter. "I want to introduce you to my friends and family, and my mom is dying to meet you."

"She is?" Jariah questioned, baffled by his words. "Why?"

"Because I told her I finally met the woman of my dreams."

Eyes wide, her heart began to beat in double time, and she swallowed hard. "You didn't…"

"I did, and there's more. You're going to be my date for my parents' anniversary bash."

"Nicco, I can't." Jariah tried not to notice his sweet, endearing smile, or the puppy-dog expression on his face. "Being your date would be career suicide."

"Baby, what are you talking about?"

Baby? Oh, God, I love the way that sounds!

Chiding herself to remain focused, she searched for the right words to make Nicco understand why she couldn't be his date for his parents' anniversary bash. Deep down, she was tickled pink that he'd invited her, but she knew attending the party with her boss would be a mistake. "If we go to the party together everyone will think that we're lovers."

"What's wrong with people knowing we're a couple? Are you ashamed of me?"

The wounded expression on his face pierced her heart. "No, of course not. You're great, and fun to be around, but I don't want our coworkers to think we're sleeping together. I want to advance my career, not ruin my reputation—"

"I would never fire you. You know that."

You won't, but Mrs. Reddick will, and I need this job!

"Why don't you ask Estelle to be your date?" Jariah said casually, though the thought of Nicco with the provocative, sex-crazed model made her burn with jealousy. "You guys make an attractive twosome, and besides, she'd look much better on your arm than I would."

Nicco stopped walking. Releasing her hand, he studied her closely as if he was seeing her for the first time. "Who's the real Jariah Brooks?" he asked, his quiet tone belying the significance of his question. "Is she the strong, tell-it-like-it-is woman I met a few months back, or is she the insecure woman standing before me who doesn't recognize her own self-worth?"

His question literally knocked the wind out of her sails. Feeling exposed, as if she was standing on the street buck naked, she lowered her eyes to the ground. Jariah had never allowed herself to be vulnerable with anyone, and although she had feelings for Nicco, she wasn't about to reveal her deepest fears to him. Not after one date. Likely, not ever. Unfortunately, he reminded her of Wesley, and Jariah knew if push ever came to shove he'd choose his family over her in a heartbeat. Guys with trust funds always did.

"I didn't mean to hurt your feelings."

"You didn't." It was a lie—his words stung, but Jariah put up a brave front. "And I'm not insecure. I just don't like people talking behind my back, and that's *exactly* what's going to happen if I accompany you to your parents' anniversary party."

Their gazes locked, zeroing in on each other like laser beams.

"Don't belittle yourself. I don't like it. You're better than that."

"Okay, so I have issues. Sue me!"

"Now, there's the strong, feisty woman I know and love."

Love? The word echoed around her head in surround sound. At the thought of spending forever with Nicco, her heart skipped a beat and danced inside her chest.

"Next Saturday is a special night for me, and the only woman I want by my side is you." He cupped her face in his hands and kissed the tip of her nose. "Got it, Ms. Brooks?"

Stunned by his bold declaration, all Jariah could do was offer a meek nod. Outwardly, she pretended as if his announcement was no big deal, as if it didn't cause her senses to go berserk. But his words floored her. *Did Nicco just say what I think he said? He'd rather go to his parents' anniversary bash with me than that gorgeous sex fiend who snuck into his office yesterday?*

"Next Friday, I'm giving you the day off."

"But we have a meeting with the Miami Capitals basketball team about a catering contract."

"I know, and I won't screw it up. I promise."

Ordering her legs to move, Jariah fell into step beside him. Keeping her wits about her was paramount. Nicco was doing what he did best—charm, seduce and entice. But she knew the Italian heartthrob had no interest in ever settling down or starting a family.

Besides, they had little in common. Jariah was a creature of habit who lived by a schedule, while Nicco liked to wing it and craved spontaneity. He loved going out, partying with his friends, but she preferred relaxing at home watching movies and reading romance novels. It was his way or the highway, and they butted heads at least once a day. Add to that his collection of freaky ex-lovers who were on call and ready to satisfy his needs faster than a New York minute. It was just a matter of time before their differences tore them apart, and she didn't want Ava to get hurt. Her daughter adored Nicco and if he walked out of her life six months down the road she'd be devastated.

"On Friday, you have a ten o'clock dress fitting at Chanel," he explained. "After lunch, you're going to Destination Wellness for some serious pampering. Think you can handle that *very* difficult assignment?"

"Nicco, I can't blow my check on spa treatments."

"I know, but I can." He flashed a sly wink. "Consider it an early birthday present."

"My birthday is six months away."

"You don't say?"

Jariah sighed. There was no use arguing with him. Stubborn and headstrong, he'd find a way to convince her and in the end she'd cave. But she wasn't sticking him with an exorbitant shopping bill. She'd pay for her outfit for the party. It was only fair. *I hope the Chanel boutique has a clearance section.*

"I feel like eating buttery popcorn." Nicco gestured at the movie theater. "You game?"

Jariah scanned the lit marquee board. "I'm not interested in seeing any of the movies playing. They're either action flicks or animations."

"I figured as much, so I planned something extraspecial for you."

"You did? What is it?"

"You'll have to wait and see."

His grin was irresistible. And when he wrapped his arms around her waist, pulling her right up to his chest, a dreamy sigh escaped her lips.

"God, you're beautiful," he praised.

The kiss came out of nowhere. At the feel of his mouth pressed firmly against hers, her body trembled, quivered and shook. Desire built, consuming her body whole. Nicco was arrogant and flamboyant, everything Jariah *didn't* want in a man, but he made her feel things she'd never experienced before—a passion so intense it paralyzed her. And his touch was divine, the best thing to ever happen to her.

They kissed in the middle of the street without a care in the world for what felt like hours. Nipping at her bottom lip, he captured it between his teeth, and gave it a flick with his tongue. "We better head inside," he said smoothly. "Our movie is about to start."

Paragon Theaters was crowded, packed to the brim with eager moviegoers, and the scent of cinnamon pretzels and nacho cheese was heavy in the air. After a trip to the concession area, Jariah had more candy than a trick-or-treater, and when Nicco ribbed her for spending all of his hard-earned money on junk food, she laughed and gave him a shot in the ribs.

Theater twelve was empty, but Nicco suggested they sit in the last row. During the previews, they chatted about dinner and fed each other Skittles. When the lights dimmed, they switched off their cell phones and made themselves comfortable.

The moment Jariah read the words that appeared on the screen, she immediately recognized the movie as *Poetic Justice.* "I can't believe they're showing this movie," Jariah said excitedly. "If I had known it was playing, I would've told my girlfriends! They love Tupac, too!"

"Baby, this is a private screening."

"A private screening?" Realization dawned, and her eyes widened. "You rented out the theater so I could watch my favorite movie?"

"Of course I did. You know I'll do anything to make you happy."

Electricity crackled in the air, and something came over Jariah. Something that made her feel feverish, wanton and sexy. Touched by his thoughtfulness and his kind, heart-felt words, Jariah leaned over and kissed his lips. A slow, lingering kiss that took Nicco by surprise. For a moment, Jariah forgot everything—the movie, her doubts, her fears about the future—and focused on pleasing the man holding her in his arms. She didn't care that they were in a movie theater or that an usher could walk in any moment and catch them making out. Jariah was going to have Nicco tonight, and nothing was going to stop her.

The spicy cologne stimulated her senses, energizing and invigorating her. Her body caught fire, and her heart beat quickened. His kisses were her weakness, his caresses her downfall. The moment his hands touched her skin, her willpower evaporated, her insides turned to mush and her nipples hardened inside her bra. Her mind and body were at war, duking it out like two heavyweight boxers in a Las Vegas ring.

And though her thoughts confused her, in the end her flesh won out. Jariah wanted a quickie—hot, fast, exhilarating sex—and Nicco was just the man to give it to her. She needed this, and if his sex was like the way he kissed, she was going to have the most explosive orgasm ever.

The lights from the movie illuminated the expression on Nicco's face. Want shone in his eyes, and his grin hinted at things to come. Reclaiming her lips, he crushed his mouth to hers. Overcome, Jariah lost count of how many times they kissed. She felt crazed, like a sex addict locked away in rehab, and yearned to feel him inside her. His kisses tasted that good, that sweet. Using the tip of his tongue, he tickled her earlobe, drew circles across her neck and licked her collarbone. Jariah felt his hand under her shirt stroking her warm, quivering skin. He cupped her breasts, and they spilled out over the top of her bra.

He fondled and caressed her breasts as if he were worshipping them, but he never took his eyes off her face. "You have beautiful breasts," he said, his expression one of awe and wonder. "They're full and luscious and perfect."

Playfully, he pinched and tweaked her nipples. Heat rushed to Jariah's core. And when Nicco trailed a finger up from her thigh to her sex and massaged her throbbing clit through her panties, she wanted to climb into his lap and ride him until he said *her* name.

Thrusting her hips against his hand, she willed him to put her out of her misery, to touch and stroke her wetness. Nicco slid a finger inside her, and then another. Moans exploded from Jariah's lips. She griped the armrest and rotated her hips. In and out, in a slow, erotic pace, his long, deft fingers worked their magic.

Exhilarated, Jariah tossed her head back and screamed her pleasure. Not once, not twice, but three ear-splitting times. It wasn't one of her finest moments, but she couldn't control her mouth or stop the tremors racking her inflamed body. The tingling sensation in her clit walloped her, pushed her to the brink. Jariah couldn't believe it, and was convinced this was nothing more than an erotic dream. But then her orgasm hit, and her body spiraled out of control, proving that her secret fantasies about her suave, sexy boss had finally come true.

Deep, savage groans fell from Jariah's lips, and several minutes passed before her legs quit trembling and the room stopped spinning around her. A heady, euphoric sensation washed over her. It made her feel light-headed, and left her unable to speak. Her mouth was dry, her lips were stuck together and her skin felt clammy and hot. Her limbs felt heavy with fatigue, but Jariah was so anxious for more she climbed onto Nicco's lap and clamped her thick thighs around his waist. "I need to feel you inside me. Here. Now," she panted, her words a desperate plea.

Straddling him, she pressed her body flat against his and massaged his broad, muscled shoulders. She stroked his chest, marveling at his chiseled upper body, and drooled over his rock-hard pecs and abs.

She buried her hands in his hair and cradled him to her chest like a mother nursing her child. He mashed her breasts together, and then slowly sucked each dark chocolate bud into his mouth. Nicco licked her nipples, kissing and nipping each one. It was a sensual, erotic game, and each flick of his tongue made Jariah moan louder and longer. Her clit was throbbing, dripping wet, and her body quivered in eager anticipation.

Pleasure built and rose to impossible heights.

"Do you have a condom in your wallet?"

"I do." The sound of his voice yanked Jariah out of her sexual haze.

Jariah dropped her gaze to his lap and licked her lips lasciviously. She unbuckled his pants, and eagerly worked her fingers over the tip of his shaft, impressed by its staggering width and length. He then pulled a condom from his wallet, removing the wrapper and sliding it down his long, thick erection.

Nicco drew his hands along her thighs, hiked up her flouncy, floral skirt and pushed aside her panties. As Jariah lowered herself onto his erection, she felt strong and sexy. Clamping her legs around him, she slowly rocked her hips back and forth.

"Damn, baby, you feel amazing. So tight and wet, I could love you like this all night."

Love me all night? Please do!

Clutching her hips in a viselike grip, he gave quick, fast thrusts. He ground himself against her clit and used his mouth and tongue to lick her earlobes. On and on it went, until Jariah was a shivering, bumbling mess. She cursed and screamed, bucked and cooed. Nicco wore a devilish grin, but never let up, only plunged deeper inside her. He alternated between slow circles and powerful thrusts that took her breath away. And just when Jariah was sure she'd had enough, he'd start the wicked, delicious pattern all over again.

His touch was divine ecstasy, as addictive as French wine. Nicco was an amazing lover, a man who knew how to arouse and please a woman, and Jariah knew that no one else would ever be able to compare to him.

Their lovemaking was wild, frenzied, but Nicco spoke in a soft, tender voice. *"Ti amo, e io sono al cento per cento pronti a impegnarsi per voi..."*

Her temperature spiked, and her body burned out of control. An insane rush of pleasure gripped her. Jariah couldn't think straight, couldn't make sense of what Nicco was saying. It couldn't possibly be true. Not after just one date, could it? He'd had too much to drink at dinner. He was tipsy, talking crazy, that had to be it. Why else would he say the words, "I love you, and I'm a hundred percent ready to commit to you," over and over again?

A shiver skidded down her spine. Jariah closed her eyes, and fought the tremors raking her damp, sweaty body. She was floating, weightless, soaring high above the clouds. Quivering, she gripped his shoulders and furiously pumped her legs like a horse jockey.

Jariah jerked and shuddered. She felt his erection growing inside her, filling her. Surrendering to her orgasm, she climaxed and collapsed like a ton of bricks against his chest. Shaken, she clung to him, panting each breath.

"Non ho mai saputo che eri un hellcat."

Raising her eyes to his face, she curled her lips in an angry pout. "I'm not a hellcat, Nicco, and just so you know, I've never, ever had sex on a first date."

"I know, baby, I'm just teasing. And just so *you* know, I loved every minute of it."

His fingers caressed her face with loving tenderness, and Jariah covered his hands with her own. It was in that moment—with their eyes locked and their bodies intertwined—that she knew, deep in her soul, that her life would never ever be the same again.

"Spend the night with me," he whispered, pressing his lips against hers. "I want to wake up tomorrow morning with you by my side."

Staring at him longingly, she felt an inaudible moan escape her lips. Jariah was anxious to get to Nicco's house, but she didn't let her excitement show on her face. Standing, she straightened her clothes, grabbed her handbag, and sashayed past him with a seductive swish of her hips. "I'm ready when you are."

Chapter 15

Yanked out of her sleep by a shrill, deafening noise, Jariah awoke and shot straight up in bed. Disorientated, she clutched the black satin sheet to her chest and glanced around at her surroundings. Her body was aching, her thoughts were cloudy and her head was pounding.

Next time, I'll drink less wine and more water.

Sunshine poured into the master bedroom through the open balcony doors, filling the space with warmth, light and fresh air. The scent of orange juice made Jariah's mouth water, and the sound of R & B music—a raunchy, explicit Robin Thicke number—made her wonder if she was, in fact, still dreaming. But then her gaze fell across the empty box of Magnum condoms on the bedside table, and she remembered her all-night sexcapade with her insatiable boss. It all came flooding back—her tryst with Nicco in the movie theater, their romantic stroll along the beach and returning to his estate in the wee hours of the morning. *Where is Nicco?*

Yawning, she swung her tired legs over the side of the bed and stretched her hands high above her head. A massage would hit the spot, and at the thought of Nicco kneading and stroking her body goose bumps erupted across her skin. It was amazing the effect he had on her, how desperate she was for him after only one night of lovemaking.

As Jariah stood, she spotted a piece of white paper lying where Nicco should have been.

I went for a run. Be back in time to make you breakfast.

Excitement and joy bubbled inside her. Only Nicco could make her feel this good, this happy. Last night, after making love for the third spellbinding time, they'd snuggled in each other's arms and talked for hours. No subject was off-limits and the crazy, outrageous stories Nicco told her about his teenage years made Jariah giggle.

Voices filled the air, drawing her gaze to the open doors. Hoping to catch sight of Nicco jogging around his estate, Jariah pushed aside the curtains, and stepped out onto the balcony. "Wow, talk about gorgeous," she gushed, shaking her head in awe.

Shielding her eyes from the sun, she marveled at the size of Nicco's opulent bachelor pad. Groundskeepers rushed about watering the lawn, trimming the shrubs and planting flowers.

Jariah heard her cell phone ring from somewhere in the master bedroom, but didn't know the first place to look. Returning inside, she frantically searched under the bed, the sitting area and the master bathroom. She couldn't find it anywhere. As she wandered around the room, trying to remember the last time she had her cell phone, Jariah noticed the outfit she wore yesterday hanging up in front of the closet door. Desperate to make love to Nicco last night, she'd tossed her sleeveless blouse and floral skirt on the floor, but to her surprise her clothes didn't look wrinkled or dirty. In fact, they looked clean, spotless.

Curious, she closed her eyes, and buried her nose in her Kate Spade blouse. It smelled like lavender fabric softener and had been ironed. *What a sweetheart!* she thought, and a girlish smile warmed her lips. Jariah wondered when Nicco had found the time to wash her clothes, and as she dressed made a mental note to thank him.

For the second time in minutes, her cell phone rang. Moving to the bed, Jariah dropped to the floor and searched around on her hands and knees. Bingo! Mrs. Covington's number appeared on the screen, but Jariah didn't panic. She knew it was Ava calling to check in, and greeted her daughter warmly. "Good morning, sweetie. How are you? Are you having a good time with Grandma and Grandpa?"

"No. I want to go home." Her voice wobbled with emotion. "I want to eat pancakes and bacon for breakfast, but Grandma said, 'no.'"

"Ava, that's no reason to cry."

"It's not my fault I'm a big-boned girl, is it, Mama? Big-boned girls are pretty, too, right?"

Jariah stared down at the phone, confused and bewildered by her daughter's words. "Honey, what are you talking about? Who said you were a big-boned girl?"

"Grandma Stella. She said big-boned people like me have no business eating bacon, and gave me a bowl of yucky oatmeal instead. Gross! I hate oatmeal."

Fighting mad, Jariah struggled to control her temper. Where did Wesley's mother get off insulting her baby? Had the woman lost her ever-loving mind? Jariah wasn't going to wait to find out. She was going to pick up Ava, and if Stella didn't like it, that was just too bad. Maybe next time she'd keep her big mouth shut and her offensive comments to herself. "Don't worry, baby girl. Everything will be fine."

"The other kids are calling me Big-Boned Ava."

"Where is Grandma Stella now?" Jariah asked through clenched teeth.

"Sitting in the sun room with her friends. They're eating brownies, but they won't let me have any," she complained.

"Ava, politely ask Grandma Stella to come to the phone."

"Are you going to come get me, Mom? I promise to be a good girl," she said. "I'll clean my room and vacuum the house…"

Jariah's heart split in two as she heard her daughter beg and plead. "I'll be there soon, I promise, but first let me talk to Grandma Stella."

"Okay. Hold on."

Jariah heard a rustling sound, boisterous female laughter, and then an eerie silence.

"Yes," Mrs. Covington drawled, sounding annoyed. "What would you like?"

"I'm coming to get Ava. Please have her ready to go in an hour."

"I will do no such thing. She is having a lovely time playing with my friends' grandkids, and is on her way to join the others in the pool."

Jariah repeated herself, speaking louder this time. "I said, I'm coming to pick up my daughter. What part of that don't you understand?"

"You can drive all the way out here if you want to but security won't let you pass through the gates. And think of how embarrassed Ava would be if you came down here and caused a scene. Is that what you want, Jariah? To embarrass your only daughter?"

Jariah wished she could reach through the phone and wring Mrs. Covington's bony neck. She thought of calling Wesley and raising hell, but knew her ex would never stand up to his mother. In his eyes, she could do no wrong. Jariah didn't care if she had to walk to the Covington estate, she was going to pick up her daughter and no one was going to stop her. "What time will your friends be leaving?"

"My book club members are staying for lunch."

"I understand." Jariah thought hard. And then she

smiled to herself as an idea came to mind. One that was guaranteed to work. "I was really hoping to take Ava to the Miami Art Museum this afternoon. The Pioneers of African-American History exhibit opens today, and I'm anxious to see it."

Stella's tone brightened. "I think that is a grand idea. Lee and I donated a million dollars to the project, and we attended the charity fundraiser, as well. Imagine how excited Ava will be when she sees our names on the gold sponsor plaque at the entrance of the exhibit."

"I was thinking the same thing," Jariah lied, rolling her eyes to the ceiling. "That's why I want to pick up Ava now. I want us to have plenty of time to explore the exhibit."

"Yes, wonderful idea, I will prepare Ava for your impending arrival."

Lady, get off it. This is not the Victorian Age, and you are no Queen Elizabeth!

"I will have her dressed and ready to go at one o'clock. Don't be late."

"Great, thank you, Mrs. Convington. See you soon."

"Park across the street when you arrive," she said, her tone losing its warmth. "Your car is an eyesore and I don't want my book club members to see it anywhere near my property."

Click.

Annoyed by the dig, Jariah swore in Italian. She stuffed her feet into her high heels, scooped up her handbag and tore out of the master bedroom. The sooner she called a cab, the sooner she could pick up Ava. Jariah wanted to see Nicco, and felt bad about leaving despite making plans to spend the day with him, but she couldn't sit around waiting for him to return from his jog. She was worried about Ava and wanted to pick her up before Wesley's mother completely shattered her self-esteem.

As Jariah descended the winding staircase, she admired

the striking decor on the main floor. In the morning light, Nicco's Coral Gables estate was even more stunning. The mansion had a modest brick exterior, but the inside was fit for a king. Oversized picture windows offered an abundance of natural sunshine and panoramic views of the Miami skyline. Decorated in rich beige and brown tones, the estate was decked out in designer furnishings and the best artwork money could buy. Brass chandeliers hung from what seemed to be every ceiling on the main floor, and a collection of Egyptian masks lined the walls. It was a dream house, one Jariah wished she could afford, and as she glanced out the window she imagined herself playing with Ava on the trampoline.

Jariah smelled the tantalizing aroma of bacon and freshly baked pastries, too, but ignored her hunger pains. Determined to make a clean getaway without running into Gerald or one of the groundskeepers, she tiptoed past the formal dining room and rushed through the grand foyer. *Almost there,* she thought, as her gaze fixed on the front door.

Her heart slammed violently against her rib cage, and her cold, clammy hands were shaking uncontrollably. As she sped passed the kitchen, someone reached out and grabbed her. Jariah shrieked, and her purse fell to the floor like a sack of potatoes.

Chuckling, Nicco wrapped her up in his arms and dropped a kiss on her cheek.

"Are you trying to kill me?" She touched a hand to her chest and breathed slowly through her nose. "You scared me half to death."

"That's what you get for trying to run off."

He turned her around to face him, and when their eyes met, Jariah felt suffocating rush of desire. Deep in her stomach, butterflies swarmed about. Her nipples hardened, strained against her bra, dying for release, and she just knew her panties were soaking wet. Nicco made her want to do wild and crazy things, and looked so damn sexy in his white T-shirt and blue running shorts, she wanted to have *him*—not Honey Nut Cheerios—for breakfast.

"Did you sleep well?" Nicco asked, blessing her with another kiss.

"Like a baby."

He laughed. "That's what I like to hear."

"How was your run?"

"Painful." His grin was sly, and his voice was undeniably erotic. "You worked me over real good last night, and I have aches and pains in places I haven't used since I was a teenager!"

His words aroused her and made her want to head back upstairs to the master bedroom for rounds four and five, but then she remembered her conversation with Ava minutes earlier, and her craving waned. "I know we made plans to have a picnic at Bayfront Park, but I have to leave," she explained, scooping her purse up off the floor. "Can you please call me a cab?"

His grin faded. "Don't go. Stay. I need you."

"You do?"

"Yeah, baby, I do." Nuzzling his face against her chin, he slipped a hand underneath her blouse and caressed the small of her back. "I'm starving. Let's go back to bed."

"Oh, so *that's* why you want me to stay." Eyeing him coolly, Jariah freed herself from his grasp. "I don't need you to walk me out. I can see myself to the door."

Nicco slid in front of her, cutting off her escape route. His features were touched with concern, and the hand he rested on her hip warmed her from the toes up.

"Baby, it's not like that," he argued, his tone as gentle as his caress. "I want you here because I love being with you. The fact that you're the best lover I've ever had is a bonus."

I'm the best lover you ever had? No way! she thought, resisting the urge to squeal.

"Sorry, Nicco, I didn't mean to snap at you." Embarrassed for overreacting, Jariah wore an apologetic smile. "I just got off the phone with Ava's grandmother, and that woman always brings the worst out in me."

"How is Ava doing? Is everything okay?"

"No, she's upset, so I'm going to pick her up early," Jariah explained, taking her cell phone out of her purse to check for missed calls. "That's why I need you to call me a cab."

"Let's go into the kitchen. You can bring me up to speed while we eat breakfast."

The glass table overlooking the deck was filled with an abundance of silver trays and juice jugs.

"Wow, your personal chef prepared quite the spread this morning."

Nicco filled a oversized plate with some of everything that was on the table. "I don't have a chef. I prefer to do all my own cooking."

"It must have taken you hours to make all of this food."

"It did, but you're worth it."

Sitting down at the table, Nicco seized Jariah around the waist and pulled her down on his lap. He picked up his fork, cut her blueberry waffle into small, tiny pieces and swirled it around in the maple syrup. "Open wide."

Jariah did and chewed slowly. Starving, she parted her lips for more. Between bites, Nicco stroked her neck, her shoulders and nibbled on her earlobes. *Who knew breakfast could be so sexy?* she thought, snuggling closer to him. He fed her until there was nothing left on her plate and dabbed her mouth with a napkin when she was finished eating.

"I could get used to this," he said, gazing up at her. "I like you being here."

I do, too. More than you know.

"I have something for you." Nicco reached into the pocket of his shorts and took out a gold key. "This is for you. I want you and Ava to come and go as you please."

"Thanks, but no thanks. I'd hate for us to bump into Estelle or one of your other exes."

"You won't."

"How can you be so sure?"

"Because you're the only woman I've ever given a key to."

Jariah felt her jaw drop, but couldn't close her gaping mouth.

"My past relationships were all superficial, short-term hookups, but I want more for us."

Fiddling with her watch strap, she avoided his searching gaze.

"What is it? Did I say something wrong?"

Silence, hung between them like a thick, dark curtain.

"Talk to me," he pleaded, taking her hands in his. "I want to know what's stopping you from trusting me. Is it my past and all of the reckless things you think I've done?"

"You come from a wealthy family, and I grew up in a low-income housing project in—"

"What does that have to do with anything?"

"I've been down this road before and I don't want to go down it again."

"I don't understand. You're talking in circles." Nicco frowned. "Is this about your ex?"

Bitter memories flooded her mind, and seconds passed before Jariah could speak.

"Ava's dad was my first love, my one and only boyfriend, and when I got pregnant three months before graduation he promised to take care of me. My parents were furious with me for having a baby out of wedlock, but I was too in love to care."

"You thought you were going to get married and live happily ever after, huh?"

"I was twenty-one, incredibly naive and believed everything would be okay as long as we loved each other."

"Sometimes love just isn't enough."

Knowing firsthand how true that was, Jariah nodded her head solemnly. "Things were going great, and I was thrilled when he asked me to move in but the minute his parents learned I was from Overtown, they started treating me differently."

"It sounds like his parents need to take a course on acceptance and sensitivity."

"I couldn't agree more. They act all high and mighty just because they have a private jet, and vacation in the Hamptons, but they are the most small-minded people I have ever met. In their eyes, I'm nothing but trash, and I'll never be good enough for their brilliant, successful son."

"Don't say things like that." His tone was one of suppressed anger, and his teeth were clenched. "You're not trash."

"Well, that's how Wesley's family made my parents feel," she confessed, her heart filled with a dull ache at the mention of her mom and dad. "Things got so bad between our families last year that my parents stopped talking to me. I got so frustrated with the situation, I sat down and wrote them a letter, but it was returned, unopened, a few weeks later."

"Keep trying. They'll come around. How could they not?" Nicco touched a hand to her cheek and kissed the corners of her lips. "You're smart and so beautiful."

"But I don't know what else to do. I've tried everything."

"Don't worry, baby, we'll think of something."

"We will?" she asked, stunned by the conviction in his voice.

"Absolutely. We're in this together, right?"

Jariah didn't speak. Tongue-tied, she didn't know what to say.

"Unless..." His face hardened like stone, and his shoulders grew stiff. "Unless you're still in love with you ex and are considering getting back together with him."

"It's not going to happen. I would never, ever take him back."

"Can I get that in writing?"

Jariah laughed. She thought Nicco was joking, but when he didn't flash his trademark grin and dodged her gaze, she realized he didn't believe her. *Why not? If anyone should be apprehensive about us dating it should be me.*

"I was willing to put up with my ex's parents, but I got sick of him giving me the runaround about our wedding," she confessed. "We were engaged for five long years, but every time I asked him to set a wedding date, he gave me one excuse after another. He had no intention of ever marrying me, so I broke things off and moved out nine months ago."

"Smart move. You deserve better."

"I think so, too."

Jariah glanced at the clock on the oven and saw that it was eleven o'clock, and she gasped. "I can't believe we've been sitting here talking for two hours," she said, standing to her feet. Quickly, she cleared the table of the dishes and put the leftovers in the fridge.

"What's the rush?" Nicco asked. He stood, picked up their empty glasses and joined her at the sink. "You have plenty of time to get to Coconut Grove."

"I know, but if I'm late, Ava's grandmother will call me a bad mother, and I'm not in the mood to hear her mouth today."

"You're an excellent mom. You know that. Don't let her get to you."

"That's easy for you to say. You've never had the misfortune of meeting her."

"True, but I have plenty of drama to deal with in my family and at the office."

"Can I ask you a personal question?"

Nicco nodded. Leaning against the counter, he folded his arms across his chest and crossed his legs at the ankles. "Ask away. I have nothing to hide."

Despite her misgivings, she asked the question that had been plaguing her thoughts from the first day she started working at Morretti Incorporated. "What happened between you and Tye Caldwell? There are rumors circulating around the office that he resigned because you slept with his wife."

He wore a dark gaze, but spoke in a calm, quiet tone. "It's not true."

"Which part? The part about Tye leaving the company or you sleeping with his wife?"

"I don't want to talk about it," he said through clenched teeth.

"I understand."

Annoyed, Jariah flung her dish towel on the counter and spun on her heels. Before she reached the breakfast bar, Nicco grabbed her waist and gathered her in his arms.

"Damn, that's not it." He hung his head and released a deep sigh. "I've never told anyone the truth about what happened with Tye."

"Why not?"

"Because it's embarrassing, and I want to forget what happened."

"Nothing you tell me will ever leave this room. I promise. You have my word."

Nicco paused, as if he was weighing the truth of her words. After a prolonged silence, he raised his head to meet her gaze, and dropped a bombshell. "Tye embezzled a million dollars from Morretti Incorporated and set me up to take the fall."

Chapter 16

Stunned, Jariah stared at Nicco with wide eyes, unable to believe his jaw-dropping confession. *His best friend had betrayed him? Why? How? When?* Dozens of questions filled her mind, but she couldn't get her thoughts in order or her lips to form a single word.

Instinctively, she moved closer to him. To comfort him, Jariah gently caressed his face. He stared off into space and when he finally spoke, the anguish in his voice brought tears to her eyes.

"I was so busy partying and enjoying the fruits of our labor that I didn't notice Tye was stealing from Dolce Vita right under my nose."

"Nicco, are you sure? Do you have proof that he was stealing from you?"

"One of the interns working in the accounting department noticed a discrepancy in the signature of a check Tye forged in my name and alerted his supervisor." Nicco laughed bitterly, and jabbed a finger at his chest. "Imagine that, a college freshman is smarter than I am!"

"Don't blame yourself. It's not your fault."

"It is," he insisted. "My family and the board of directors also think so."

"I don't care what they think," Jariah argued. "They're wrong. Tye was your best friend. You had every right to trust him."

Nicco hung his head and raked a hand through his hair. His shoulders were hunched in defeat and worry lines creased his forehead. "I knew something was up with Tye, but I didn't want to believe that my best friend would ever screw me over."

"Why did he do it? Was he in financial trouble?"

"No, he got greedy." His narrowed eyes appeared dark. "Tye was never satisfied, and spent money like it was growing on trees. He was always competing with me, but I didn't care. Business was booming, and at the time I felt I owed the success of Dolce Vita to him."

"Seeing your best friend locked up must have been hard on you."

"Tye's not in jail. Last I heard he was backpacking through Europe."

"Why didn't you go to the police and have him arrested?"

Anguish covered his face and seeped into his voice. "Because Tye was more than just a friend and a business partner. He was my brother."

"But he lied and betrayed your trust."

"Italians are incredibly loyal people, and nothing matters more to me than the happiness of my friends and family," he said, wearing a sad smile. "I couldn't let Tye go to jail, so I repaid the money he stole and forced him to resign. He caused a scene at the office, even threatened to kill me, but it was all for show. Tye wanted to save face, but we both know I did him a favor."

"Where's his family now? Are they in Europe, too?"

"No, they're here in Miami. The past twelve months

have been tough on Meredith and Richie, but they're hanging in there."

"Richie, your godson. Of course, now everything makes sense," Jariah said, as all the pieces of the puzzle fit together. "You're his surrogate dad now that Tye's gone."

"I'm trying, but I have a lot to learn. Meredith said if I don't toughen up, Richie's going to walk all over me. But it's hard to say no to such a cute, smooth-talking kid!"

As they chatted about Ava and Richie, they loaded the dishwasher and wiped down the counters. Once the kitchen looked spic and span, Jariah grabbed her purse and put on her jacket.

"I wish you didn't have to go. I love having you here," he said in a hushed whisper. Nicco tipped her head back and stared deep into her eyes. "I've fallen hard for you, Jariah. I hate when we're apart."

Something inside Jariah told her that he was telling the truth, but her doubts still plagued her troubled thoughts. One kiss was all it took to make her melt. Back in his arms, his hands linked around her waist, Jariah realized there was nowhere in the world she'd rather be. Nicco nibbled on her bottom lip. Her nipples hardened under her blouse, aching for his lips, his teeth and his nimble tongue.

"You can trust me with your heart. I won't ever hurt you or mistreat you…"

His words gave her reassurance. And when he cupped her face in his hands and kissed her passionately on the lips, Jariah knew deep in her heart that Nicco Morretti was the man she'd been waiting for her whole life.

"Baby, you have no idea what you do to me," he said, his voice hoarse. "I love you with all my heart, and I want a chance to prove that I'm the only man you need."

Jariah parted her lips and blurted out the question on the tip of her tongue. "You want to get married?"

"Are you proposing?"

"No, silly," she said, laughing. "I just want to know if marriage is on the table."

"Absolutely." Nicco dropped his gaze to her breasts and licked his lips. "I love the idea of you being my wife and coming home to you after a hard day's work. You are, without a doubt, the sweetest piece of chocolate I have ever tasted, and I'm hungry for you right now."

"But what if you change your mind about us? Or meet a gorgeous video girl when you're in L.A. at the end of the month? Where would that leave me?"

"Jariah, nothing is ever going to come between us. You're my heart, and I've found something in you that I've never found in anyone." Nicco gripped her hips, and rubbed his groin against her. The muscles bulging in his arms weren't the only thing rock hard. "And why would I want a skanky video girl when I have a little vixen like you waiting for me at home?"

"Why indeed?" Jariah quipped, batting her eyelashes.

Hungrily, he covered her mouth with his. His lips against hers was a heady feeling Jariah could never, ever tire from. "Nicco, stop," she panted, pressing her hands flat against his chest to keep him at bay. "What if one of the groundskeepers walks in on us?"

"Haven't you ever fantasized about having sex on the kitchen table?"

A soft moan escaped her lips. "Sex is like real estate, baby. It's all about location, and I'm going to do you right here, right now." His lips nipped at her earlobe, and his hands fondled her breasts. "And you don't have to worry about anyone interrupting us. Gerald is under strict orders not to let anyone inside the house while you're here."

His mouth covered hers, and her protest died on her lips. Weakened by his kiss, she sank against his chest and buried her hands in his hair. Jariah was turned on by his urgent caress and his deep, guttural groans.

Nicco pushed a hand under her skirt and slid two fingers inside her panties. Gently, he parted the swollen, fleshly lips between her legs. Breathless, she quivered. A shudder ripped through her, and her knees threatened to give way. Instinctively, she arched her body toward him, and returned his deep, sensuous kiss.

His tongue aroused her, and each flick of his fingers electrified her. To give him deeper access, she parted her legs, spreading them wide.

Quickening his pace, he flicked his wrist harder, pumping it vigorously inside her. His furious speed left her teetering on the edge of delirium. Cursing in Italian, she grabbed fistfuls of his hair and rocked her hips powerfully against his hands.

Her eyes fluttered closed, and an ear-splitting scream fell from her lips. Jariah couldn't get a handle on her emotions that were spiraling out of control, and felt the impulse to cry. His stroke was that intense.

Spasms stabbed her spine, racked her trembling, overheated body. Her legs buckled, and when he whipped off her blouse and closed his mouth around a nipple, Jariah threw her head back in ecstasy.

Their hands, and lips and bodies found sweet solace in each other, a passion she had never known. They staggered around the kitchen, stumbling into appliances and furniture as if they were in the dark. Nicco backed Jariah up against the kitchen table and turned her toward the window. She parted her legs, opened wide like a flower in bloom. He stroked and massaged her clit until delicious tremors rocked her body.

"Enough! I need you inside me now!"

"I love when you get mad. It's so primitive and sexy."

Tossing a coy grin over her shoulder, she swiveled her butt against his crotch.

"Don't start something you can't finish," he warned.

Nicco then slapped her lightly on the bottom, and when a moan fell from her lips, he did it again. They played and teased, kissed and laughed, and by the time he put on the condom he'd grabbed from his secret stash underneath the utensil drawer, and slid his erection inside of her, she'd had two explosive orgasms.

Nicco gave slow, calculated thrusts, as if it was her first time and he didn't want to hurt her. Love filled her heart and tears came to her eyes. Nothing had ever felt so right. Being loved by Nicco was everything Jariah had ever dreamed of and more. Completely in sync, they moved together as one, their bodies swaying to the inaudible beat of their hearts.

He trailed kisses down her neck, lovingly caressing and stroking her hips. Nicco was breathing heavily, but he moved in a slow, measured pace like he had all the time in the world. His stroke was divine, exquisite, and filled every inch of her.

"Kiss me." His words were an urgent command, and seeing the desire in his eyes made Jariah feel like the most beautiful woman in the world. Their lips touched, and their tongues lapped desperately against each other. Convulsing uncontrollably, she felt herself unraveling, and knew she was falling apart. Moaning and groaning at a deafening pitch, she feared if she screamed again the groundskeepers would run in.

"Don't fight it, baby. Let go…let go." Nicco plunged inside her deeper than ever before. Lust infected his body like a virus. He ran his hands down her shoulders, gliding them over her tight, perfectly round butt. *What a view!* Jariah had curves for days, and the most beautiful ass he'd ever seen. The sex was outstanding, without question the best he'd ever had, but that was not what he liked most about her. She was more than just a pretty face; she was honest and trustworthy. The more time they spent together the deeper he fell in love. He wanted a future with her and could picture her living with him in his Coral Gables mansion. He knew that one day soon she'd become Mrs. Nicco Morretti. But first, he had to tell her the truth about—

A door slammed, and footsteps pounded on the tile floor, which jarred Nicco from his thoughts. He heard laughter in the distance, and instantly recognized the voices of the intruders. *Son of a bitch!* His brothers were in his house, and if he didn't move fast they were going to see the woman he loved buck naked.

"Oh, my, goodness, someone's inside the foyer!" Jariah straightened, slipped her blouse back on and adjusted her skirt in record time. "This is so embarrassing. What if this gets back to the office?"

"It's not my staff. It's my brothers. I guess they caught an earlier flight."

The color drained from her face and fear flashed in her big, brown eyes.

"Baby, relax," he said, kissing her lips, "my brothers are going to love you."

Jariah frantically combed her hair with her fingertips. "Do I look okay?"

"You look sensational, and if I had my way you'd still be spread wide-open on my—"

Behind him, someone cleared their throat.

Nicco turned and saw his brothers standing at the entrance of the kitchen, and he smothered a groan. He was annoyed by their untimely arrival, but didn't show it. Casually dressed in T-shirts, khaki shorts and dark aviator sunglasses, they could easily pass for a couple of rich college students on summer vacation. "Hey, guys, it's good to see you. How was your flight?"

Demetri and Rafael exchanged worried glances, but didn't speak.

The silence in the air was suffocating.

"We've been calling and texting you for hours to update you about our flight schedule," Demetri said, taking off his sunglasses. "Did you lose your phone again?"

"I switched it off last night and forgot to turn it back on," he said, wearing a wry smile. "To be honest, I don't even know where it is!"

Rafael grunted. "Why doesn't that surprise me? It's obvious you've been *occupied*."

Nicco heard the bitter edge in his brother's tone, but disregarded it. "This beautiful young woman is Jariah Brooks," he said, taking her hand in his and giving it a light squeeze. "Baby, these are my brothers, Rafael and Demetri."

"Jariah Brooks? You're new executive assistant?" Rafael folded his arms across his chest. The whites of his eyes doubled their size. "What the hell is going on here?"

"It's none of your business bro, stay out of it."

"I—I—I should go," Jaraiah stammered. "It's almost one o'clock."

Nicco could almost see the tension radiating off her body. To assure her that everything was fine, he shot her a playful wink. But it didn't work. She bit her bottom lip and nervously shuffled her feet.

"It's a pleasure to meet you both." Jariah slipped on her high heels and collected her things from the breakfast bar. "I have to go pick up Ava. I'll talk to you later."

"I'll drive you to Coconut Grove. It's not far from here."

"No, don't, stay with your brothers. I'll be fine."

"You're too stubborn for your own good," he grumbled, opening the side drawer beside the fridge and grabbing a set of keys. "Take the Mercedes. It's parked right out front."

Shaking her head, she waved her hands frantically in the air. "No way! You just bought it a few weeks ago and the rims costs more than my car!"

"Don't argue. Just take it. It's yours until your car is fixed."

Jariah hesitated. "Are you sure?"

"I'm positive." Nicco pressed the keys into her palm. "I'll walk you out."

Ignoring the shell-shocked expressions on his brothers' faces, he led Jariah out of the kitchen.

Outside, seconds later, he crouched down beside the driver's-side door, and gave her a rundown of the controls.

"I hate to see you go," Nicco said, stroking her long, silky brown legs. He could hear the desperation in his voice, but he wanted her to stay, and wasn't too proud to beg. "Why don't you pick up Ava and come back here? I'll fire up the grill, put on some Taylor Swift and we'll have a grand time."

Jariah laughed. "Ava would love that! She's obsessed with that girl!"

"I know, last Sunday when Richie and I were over for dinner, she sang us a bunch of Taylor's songs." Nicco smiled at the memory, wondering when the spunky six-year-old had captured his heart. "Every time I think of Ava using the remote as a microphone, I crack up."

"Maybe we can barbecue another time, though," Jariah said. "I'm taking Ava to the museum this afternoon, and I have to teach a self-defense class at five o'clock."

"Then I'll swing by later, and take you lovely ladies out for gelato."

"Aren't you going to hang out with your brothers tonight?"

"My fridge is stocked. They can survive without me for an hour or two."

Her eyes brightened. "All right, I accept."

"Great. I'll pick you ladies up at seven o'clock."

Nicco cupped her chin and hungrily devoured her mouth. Minutes passed as they feasted on each other's lips. Jariah finally pulled away, but when Nicco saw the time on the dashboard clock, he stood and closed the driver's-side door. "Drive safe, beautiful. I'll see you later."

"Definitely." She put on her sunglasses and waved. "Thanks for everything, Nicco."

Nicco stood in the driveway, watching Jariah cruise down the street in his new Mercedes.

"What the hell has gotten into you?"

"I should be asking you the same question." Nicco turned around and stared down his older brother. "You were way out of line, and I don't like the way you spoke to my girl."

"Son of a bitch!" Rafael shouted, throwing his hands up in the air. "Didn't you learn anything from the incident with Gracie?"

"Yeah, I did," he shot back. "I learned that you think I'm the scum of the earth."

"I never said that."

"You didn't have to. The minute Gracie cried sexual harassment you convinced dad to pay her off. You never once asked me if the allegations were true."

"That's because you have a track record of thinking with your dick *instead* of your head."

Nicco flinched as if he'd been slapped. His brother's words stung, cut him to the quick. "Not this time. Jariah isn't just any girl."

"What makes her so special?"

"Everything. She's honest, smart as hell and she's not afraid to call me out when I mess up. Hell, sometimes I think it's her favorite pastime!"

Nicco chuckled, but noticed his brother remained stoic. But he didn't care if Rafael believed him. He'd finally met his dream woman, and he wasn't going to let anyone ever come between them.

"Who's Ava?" Raphael asked.

"Jariah's six-year-old daughter."

"When did you start dating single moms?"

On the surface, Nicco remained calm, but inside he was doing a slow burn. Anger surged through his veins, and his hands balled into tight fits. He wanted to pummel Rafael's face into the ground, but he cracked his knuckles instead.

"You have no business dating a woman with a kid."

The veins in his neck twitched and throbbed uncontrollably.

"You're an adrenaline junky who gets off on breaking the rules. It's just a matter of time before you get bored and move on to greener pastures."

Nicco shot his brother a disgusted look.

"Does she know about Gracie?"

"No, not yet. I'm waiting for the right time to tell her."

"There's never a right time to tell a woman you were accused of sexual harassment," he said. "I'm going to keep my mouth shut for now, but you better hope dad doesn't find out about your office affair."

"Don't worry, I plan to introduce Jariah to mom and dad as soon as they get to town."

"Well, I'll be damned." Rafael whistled. "I can't believe you're actually serious about this girl. Hell, next you'll be telling me you're ready to tie the knot!"

A grin overwhelmed his mouth, one that caused him to feel like a kid again. "Think mom and dad will mind if I pop the question next Saturday at their anniversary bash?"

"Next Saturday!" Rafael shouted, his eyes bulging straight out of his head. "Slow your roll. You guys just met. You hardly know each other."

"I want Jariah to know that I love her, and I'm ready to commit—"

"Then buy her a promise ring."

"A promise ring isn't going to cut it. She's twenty-seven, not sixteen."

"This is too much drama to deal with on an empty stomach," Rafael grumbled, scowling. "I'm going inside. I need a shot of Patrón."

Chapter 17

"Are you ready to make our grand entrance, Mrs. Nicco Morretti-to-be?"

A giggle tickled Jariah's throat. She glanced up from her compact mirror, saw Nicco watching her and dropped it back inside her purse. "Don't you think you're getting ahead of yourself?" she asked, meeting his gaze head-on. "We haven't known each other long."

"When a man knows, he knows, and I knew the moment I laid eyes on you that you were the only woman for me."

"Was that before or after I insulted you?"

Nicco chuckled. The sound of his thick, husky laugh made Jariah feel downright giddy. He knew just what to say to make her melt, and sitting alone with him in the close quarters of the Rolls Royce limousine was wreaking havoc on her mind and body.

Staring down at her hands, Jariah admired her bright, multicolored nails. Ava had selected the design, and as she thought about the mother-daughter manicures they'd received that afternoon at Glamour Girlz, a smile warmed her heart. After they left the salon, they'd met Nicco for lunch. Every time Jariah thought about what Ava had told him during dessert she giggled.

"I like you," she'd announced, shoveling chocolate ice-cream into her mouth. "You're sweet and funny, and you always make my mommy laugh."

"Thanks, Ava. I think you're pretty cool, too."

"You can live with us if you want."

Nicco had cocked an eyebrow. "I can?"

"Yes, but only if you bring Richie. He's my new BFF!"

Car horns honked, drawing Jariah's gaze outside. The limousine was parked in front of Dolce Vita and dozens of couples, decked out in ball gowns, designer suits and top hats flocked inside the five-star restaurant. A red carpet scattered with rose petals flowed down the sidewalk, and waiters offered each new arrival a glass of champagne.

Peering out the tinted windows, Jariah spotted several Morretti Incorporated employees walking up the street arm-in-arm. The female interns looked young and stylish in their colorful dresses. The sound of their girlish laughter carried on the evening breeze.

"I'm so nervous, I'm shaking," Jariah confessed, fiddling with the three-stone diamond pendant at her neck. Nicco had given it to her hours earlier, and it was still hard to believe he'd spent thousands of dollars on her at the Cartier boutique. It was the most beautiful piece of jewelry Jariah had ever seen, and she was deeply touched by the sweet, unexpected gift. "What if my coworkers turn against me for being your date?" she asked, giving voice to her fears. "What if Mrs. Reddick causes a scene during cocktail hour? Or fires me on the spot?"

"Jariah, you have nothing to worry about. I won't leave your side."

"Can I get that in writing?" she joked, using his favorite line.

"You don't need to. You have my word."

To calm her nerves, Jariah took a long, deep breath. It didn't help, and the more she tried to relax, the harder her legs shook. The raspberry-colored, one-shoulder gown she'd eagerly purchased weeks earlier at Macy's now felt tight enough to choke her. "Do I look okay? Are you sure my dress isn't too tight?"

"You look incredible, and I can't wait to show you off to my family and friends." Touching her face, he sprayed kisses across her nose and cheeks. His voice was intimate, as gentle as a feather along her spine. "We're going to celebrate this joyous occasion with my parents, and after the party wraps up I'm taking you back to my place for dessert."

His grin was her weakness, his touch her Kryptonite. And when his gaze slid down her hips Jariah knew exactly what he had on his mind. They desperately wanted the same thing. But she played coy and teased him with a wink and a salacious look. "What's on the menu?"

"You'll have to wait and see."

The back door swung open, and a spicy, piquant fragrance flooded the limousine. Stars specked the night sky, the evening breeze whipped wildly through the trees, and music blared from the fleet of luxury cars parked along Biscayne Boulevard.

Nicco stepped out of the limousine and offered his right hand. He drew her into his arms, and pressed his mouth against hers. Their eyes connected, and when he smiled at her—one of his slow, easy, grins—Jariah felt a deep sense of peace. And just like that, her body quit shaking and her ears stopped throbbing. Being in Nicco's arms would never grow old. She gloried in their newfound love, relished every minute they spent together, and was hopeful about their future. Who cared what anyone else had to say? Why did it matter? She was in a committed relationship with a wonderful man who adored her daughter, and she wasn't going to let anyone come between them.

"Sei una bellezza vivace, e io sono completamente e irrimediabilmente colpita con voi."

His words caused her fears to dissipate and her confidence to soar. "You're right. I *am* a vivacious beauty." Feeling playful and sexy, she raised her chin, arched her shoulders and struck pose. "You're one *very* lucky man, Nicco Morretti!"

Flashing his trademark grin, he slid his hands down her back, and squeezed her butt. "I couldn't have said it better myself, now, let's go party!"

The Dolce Vita dining room was a scene of gaiety and excitement. And when Jariah saw the satin-draped ceilings, towering flower vases overflowing with long-stemmed roses and the eight-tiered wedding cake covered in sparkling gems she knew Nicco and his brothers had spared no expense for their parents' twenty-fifth wedding anniversary.

Round tables draped with silver tablecloths were covered with fine china and floating candles that showered the room with a sultry, golden hue. Backed by a ten-piece orchestra, a blue-eyed, soul crooner entertained guests as they sipped champagne, and feasted on imported caviar. The silver and red decor was striking, the music was enchanting and the air was filled with an appetizing aroma.

"What do you think?" Nicco asked as they entered the dining room.

"I've never seen anything like this. It's incredible, but a little over-the-top."

"That's what I was hoping you'd say!" Chuckling, he pecked her on the cheek. "My mom loves throwing big parties, so I told Claudia to go all-out, and she delivered big-time."

"You can say that again," Jariah agreed. "I don't know what you're paying her, but she's worth every penny."

He dropped his mouth to her ear. "Maybe we should hire her to plan our wedding."

"Don't we have to get engaged first?"

"How does tonight sound?"

Jariah tried not to faint, but just the thought of marrying Nicco and becoming his lawfully wedded wife made her feel light-headed. "I don't need a party planner. I just want a simple, elegant wedding with my friends and family."

"That's it? You don't want a lavish venue or a five-page guest list?"

"Nicco, if you're by my side, I'll have everything I'll ever need."

He pressed a kiss to her lips, and she snuggled against his chest. Deep inside, Jariah could feel herself changing, growing and becoming a stronger, more confident woman. It was hard to believe that one man could change her, but the Italian-born businessman had. In Nicco, she'd found what she'd been looking for her whole life. Their personalities meshed well, they always had a blast together and they shared the same values and beliefs. Feeling content for the first time in months, she slid her arms around his waist and returned his kiss.

During cocktail hour, they socialized with guests, posed for pictures in front of the ice sculpture and fed each other oysters and tropical fruit. Walking around the restaurant on Nicco's arm was an intoxicating feeling. He introduced her to his relatives, proudly showed her off to his business associates and kept a protective arm around her waist. Meeting the mayor was a treat, but nothing topped slow-dancing with Nicco to her favorite Michael Bublé song.

At seven o'clock, the lights dimmed, and guests donned elaborate party masks and colored beads in honor of the couple's New Orleans wedding ceremony twenty-five years earlier.

"Our guests of honor will be here in twenty minutes," Claudia Jeffries-Medina announced, clapping her hands together to capture the attention of the audience. A hush fell over the dining area, and all heads turned to the bubbly party planner. "I just received word that Mr. and Mrs. Morretti have left Country Club Miami, so everyone, please get in place…"

Gerald appeared, spoke quietly to Nicco and took off like a thief in the night.

"I have a surprise for you," Nicco said, draping an arm around her shoulder.

"Again? But we had a quickie in the office ten minutes ago."

He grinned. "I know *you're* not complaining. You begged for more!"

Nicco led Jariah through the dining room and out into the waiting area. And there, standing beside the aquarium, were her parents. They were dressed in formal designer threads, which made them look years younger.

"Mom, Dad, oh, my goodness, it's so great to see you!" Jariah threw her arms around her parents and held them tight. Her dad kissed her on the forehead, and her eyes stung and burned. Feeling his love caused the tears she'd been holding inside for the past eight months to finally break free. "I've missed you guys so much."

"Honey, don't cry. You're going to ruin your makeup, and you look so pretty." Mrs. Brooks snatched the handkerchief out of her husband's jacket pocket and cleaned her daughter's tear-stained cheeks. "We didn't want to stand in the way of your happiness, so after you sent that email we decided to stay away—"

Jariah cut in. "Mom, what are you talking about? What email?"

Mrs. Brooks spoke openly about how hurtful the message was, and confessed that she'd cried herself to sleep for weeks afterward.

"What? That's crazy. I never sent that message."

"You didn't?" Mrs. Brooks asked.

"Never. Someone must have hacked into my email."

Mr. Brooks frowned and stroked his freshly trimmed black beard. "But the message was full of personal, private details only you would know."

Or, someone close to me, Jariah thought, her brain switching into overdrive. Her heart beat raced, pounded with anger. The truth came to her, hit her like a ton of bricks. She thought back to months earlier to the day she'd dumped Wesley, and as his insults played in her mind. She knew he'd to have been the one to send the bogus email to her parents. He knew her email password, had access to her laptop and had never hid his dislike for her mom and dad.

Emotion clogged Jariah's throat, making it impossible for her to speak. Later, when they were alone, she'd share her suspicions with her parents, but now was neither the time nor the place. Not with Nicco standing behind her, listening in. The less he knew about her ex the better.

"I know we've had our differences in the past, and haven't always see eye-to-eye, but I would never intentionally hurt you. I love you guys, and not being able to see you has been torture."

"That's what Nicco said when he came by the house yesterday."

Bewildered, Jariah eyed Nicco. "You went to Overtown to meet my parents?"

"I had to. I wanted them here to celebrate with us tonight."

"Honey, we're so proud of you," Mrs. Brooks said, beaming from ear-to-ear. "Nicco told us you're the best executive assistant he's ever had!"

"You're proud of me? Really? Even though I've made so many mistakes?"

Mr. Brooks rested a hand on his daughter's shoulder. "Mistakes are what make us human. We haven't always agreed with your decisions, but we have never stopped loving you."

Jariah's vision blurred with tears, but she told herself not to cry. In that moment, standing beside Nicco and her parents, something inside her lifted. And as she listened to her father praise her accomplishments, she couldn't wipe the smile off her face.

"You're an outstanding mother and a thoughtful daughter," he continued.

"I still can't believe you booked us the penthouse suite at the Shore Club. We have our own butler *and* a free mini bar!" Mrs. Brooks exclaimed. "And the Macy's shopping spree this afternoon was amazing!"

Jariah turned to Nicco and mouthed the words *Thank you.* She realized she couldn't love him more. He walked as if he owned the world, but beneath the cocky attitude was a sensitive, loving man with a heart of gold. And Jariah loved him, mind, body and soul.

The front doors swung open, and hot air blew inside the waiting area.

"I thought this was a classy, sophisticated party. What are *you* doing here?"

Jariah heard Stella Covington's haughty voice and spun around with a stinging retort on her lips. But before she could get the words out, Nicco gave Mrs. Covington a hug, and kissed her on both cheeks. "Mr. and Mrs. Covington, I'm glad you made it, and just in time, my parents should be arriving any minute…"

Nicco knows The Covingtons? Her stomach lurched violently from left to right. Of course he did. They were a powerhouse couple, one of the wealthiest in Miami. See-

ing Nicco with them reminded Jariah that he was *way* out
of her league.

With her pulse pounding, she watched as Nicco laughed
and chatted with the Covingtons. It was sweltering outside, easily ninety degrees, but Stella was wearing a fur
shawl, a vintage lace floor-length dress, and what had to
be a million dollars in diamonds.

"What are you doing here?" Mrs. Covington demanded,
flipping her hair over her shoulders. "Shouldn't you be at
home caring for Ava?"

Nicco stepped forward, and draped an arm possessively
around her waist. "Baby, you never told me you knew the
Covingtons."

"Y-y-you're dating?" Mrs. Covington's face was as pale
as her gown. "Why doesn't that surprise me? You've always had a penchant for wealthy men, haven't you, Jariah?"

The silence was so awkward, Jariah imagined herself
crashing through the emergency exit and diving back inside the Rolls Royce. Her impulse was to run, but before
she could make a break for it, Nicco tightened his hold,
so close she couldn't move. She expected him to question
her, to ask her if the accusations were true, but he didn't.
He only smiled and gave her a peck on the lips.

"Let's head back inside. My parents should be here
any minute."

"Nicco, you don't know that girl like I do. She's sneaky
and conniving—"

"Who the hell are you calling conniving?" Mrs. Brooks
demanded, placing a hand to her broad hips. "Mind your
tongue, Stella, or I'll slap you into next week!"

Tempers flared, insults flew, and all hell broke loose.
The couples were arguing so loudly, no one saw Mr. and
Mrs. Morretti enter the waiting area. "What is going on
here?"

Jariah winced and hung her head. Mr. and Mrs. Morretti looked shell-shocked, like the sole survivors of a ship wreck, and worse, her mom had kicked off her high heels, and was taking off her clip-on earrings.

"Nicco, answer me, what is going on?" Though short and stout, with a full head of gray hair, Mr. Morretti had an air of authority and a commanding presence.

"Arturo, I'll tell you what's going on." Mrs. Covington used one hand to smooth her disheveled hair, and the other to adjust her gown. "That *girl* has been cheating on my Wesley with your son, and had the nerve to show up here with her vulgar, ill-mannered parents!"

"Vulgar?" Mrs. Brooks wagged a finger in the socialite's face. "I'll show you vulgar!"

Mrs. Brooks lunged at Mrs. Covington, but Mr. Brooks grabbed her around the waist and whisked her over to the black leather couch before she could land a single blow. "That's enough," he snapped. "You've said your peace, now let it go. You're embarrassing Jariah..."

"I refuse to break bread with uncouth factory workers from Overtown," Mrs. Covington spat, folding her arms across her chest. "If they don't leave, then I will."

Mrs. Morretti shook her head, and linked arms with Mrs. Covington. "You're not going anywhere, Stella. I haven't seen you in ages, and we have tons of catching up to do."

Mrs. Covington wore a victorious smile.

"Put this ugly incident behind you, and join me inside for cocktails." Mrs. Morretti glared at Jariah. Anger showed on her face, and her dark eyes were filled with disgust. "You and your parents aren't welcome here, so please leave, or I will call the police."

"She's not going anywhere." Nicco clasped Jariah's hand. "Jariah's my date, and I personally invited her parents—"

Arturo frowned. "Your date for what? And why is the restaurant in complete darkness?"

"Deborah, let's go. I don't want to stay where I'm not welcome, and if we hurry I can catch the second half of the baseball game." Mr. Brooks took his car keys out of his jacket pocket. "Baby girl, are you coming with us?"

Jariah's mouth dried, and her temples throbbed. Time stood still for what seemed like an eternity. Her throat was so sore, it hurt to swallow. Everyone was staring at her. She could sense it, feel it, knew they all were watching her every move. Shifting from one foot to the next, she struggled with what to do.

"Jariah, si prega di rimanere. Ho bisogno di te al mio fianco questa sera."

Her stomach did a triple back flip into her throat, but when Nicco stroked her forearm her heart melted. His voice was octaves lower, and his gaze was a light caress across her face. Jariah wanted to spend the rest of the night dancing with Nicco and stealing kisses inside the vintage photo booth, but she couldn't risk hurting her parents again.

"Have a great time with your family, Nicco, and thanks for everything."

"Baby, don't go. You have as much right to be here as anyone else."

Her sadness sat on her chest like a fifty-pound boulder. In a perfect world, it wouldn't matter where she was from, or that she'd had a child out of wedlock, but tonight it did. Especially to people like Stella Covington. Jariah would rather go home with her parents than spend another minute in the socialite's ugly presence. "Good night."

Her mind made up, she turned away from Nicco and linked arms with her mom and dad. As they exited Dolce Vita, tears coursed down Jariah's cheeks, staining her designer gown.

Chapter 18

"What are you doing up so early? On Sundays, you never crawl out of bed before noon, and when you do it's usually kicking and screaming!"

Nicco chuckled, but he didn't find anything funny about his dad cracking jokes on him at six in the morning. He was surprised—shocked actually—to see his mom cleaning the microwave, and his dad sitting at the table reading the newspaper. The very table he and Jariah had made love on just days earlier. Images of her naked, curvy body bombarded his mind, causing an erection to swell inside his jeans. He could still hear her moans, smell the perfume of her sex, and he wondered if he'd ever be able to look at Jariah and not want to make love to her.

Changing the channel in his mind, he joined his dad at the kitchen table and dropped down into the nearest chair. Nicco knew what was coming next, but was determined not to lose his temper. His parents always stayed at his Coral Gables estate when they were in Miami, but this was the first time they'd ever taken over his kitchen. They jokingly referred to his guest quarters as their "love shack," and would stay cooped up inside the plush, all-white suite for days on end. So seeing them in his space put Nicco on high alert. They were up to something. No doubt about it. Last night, during dinner, gossip-loving Stella Covington had probably filled his mother's head with filthy lies about Jariah, and now, armed with misinformation, she was anxious to talk. And so was he.

At the thought of Jariah, he felt an overpowering rush of emotion. He couldn't stop smiling or thinking about her, and he looked forward to seeing her that afternoon. Last night, after the anniversary bash ended, he'd driven over to Jariah's townhome. Inside the living room, they'd had an open, honest conversation. One that lasted for hours.

He told her about what happened with Gracie, and she told him about her tumultuous relationship with Wesley, and her ongoing struggle to keep the peace for their daughter's sake. Sharing their past pain and disappointments made Nicco feel even closer to Jariah. He was not only prepared to defend her, he was ready to propose to her. But first, he had to set the record straight with his parents.

Right on cue, his mother closed the microwave, and dropped her dishrag on the counter. Mr. Morretti lowered his newspaper and stared at Nicco over the rim of his Armani eyeglasses.

The tension in the room was suffocating.

"Thanks for making breakfast, Ma. Everything looks good," Nicco said, admiring the delicious spread. Helping himself to a plate, he loaded it with all of his favorites. "Ma, why do you look so glum? Didn't you have a good time at your anniversary bash last night?"

Her brown eyes filled with gratitude. "I had a wonderful time, but that altercation with that girl and her parents is still weighing on my mind."

"Altercation? You make it sound like they assaulted you." Nicco took a healthy bite of his panini and chewed slowly. "Mrs. Brooks's anger was directed at Mrs. Cov-

ington, not you. They have a sordid history, and if everything Jariah told me is true, Mrs. Covington has made
their lives a living hell."

"I find that very hard to believe. I've known Stella and
Lee Covington for years, and they're one of the most charitable and generous couples I know."

Mr. Morretti folded his newspaper and set it aside. "Listen to your mother, son. She knows what she's talking
about."

"And I know Jariah. She's loyal, honest and I trust her
completely."

"Is that why you gave the little tart your Mercedes?"

He took offence to his mother's quip, but didn't speak
on it. "Jariah needed a car, and I have plenty, so I insisted
she take one. Ask Rafael and Demetri. I had to practically
force the keys into her hands."

"Right, good one." His father gave a harsh, bitter laugh.
"Who would want to drive around town in a brand-new,
custom-designed Mercedes? I know I wouldn't!"

"What if she damages your car? Or sells it to a chop-
shop?" Mrs. Morretti questioned, her voice full of fear and
fret. "What then? Could you imagine the scandal? We'd be
the laughingstock of the country club and Miami's High
Society league."

"Jariah would never do that. She's not that kind of person."

"How the hell do you know? You've only known her
for five minutes!" Mr. Morretti struck his fist on the table.
The noise reverberated around the room, causing the plates
and utensils to rattle. "I knew this was going to happen.
That's why I told Mrs. Reddick to hire a male assistant to
work with you. If that girl goes to the tabloids or screams
rape it will ruin us, and I've worked too damn hard and
too damn long to watch everything I've worked tirelessly
for go up in smoke."

Shaking his head, he refuted his father's claim. "Dad, you have nothing to worry about. Jariah would never do anything to hurt me or to betray my trust. She loves me and I love her."

"Open your eyes, son, it's all an act. You're her meal ticket to a better future, and if you're not careful she'll betray you just like Gracie did, and Tye…"

Too tired to argue, he blocked out their voices and finished eating his breakfast. He snuck a glance at the clock, saw that it was ten o'clock, and took a swig of his orange juice. It was time to go. He was taking Ava and Richie to the movies, and he didn't want to be late.

"So, how long have you been screwing Mrs. Brooks?"

Nicco winced, as if he had a sore tooth, and dropped his fork on his plate. He glared at his father, staring him dead in the eye. His dad looked amused. Out of his two brothers, he looked the most like Arturo, and if that wasn't bad enough he'd also inherited his father's sharp tongue, and pessimistic nature. Before meeting Jariah, he'd thought the worst of people, and didn't trust anyone outside of his inner circle. But he didn't feel that way anymore. He'd finally found his better half, the woman he was destined to grow old with and he wasn't going to let his father reduce their relationship to meaningless sex. "I love Jariah with all my heart and I'm going to marry her."

"Nicco, you will not marry that girl. I forbid it."

"Ma, quit calling her *that girl*," he snapped, finally reaching his breaking point. "Her name is Jariah, and I'm going to propose on her birthday, so you better get on board fast."

"But she's from Overtown, and—"

Disappointed, Nicco hung his head and dragged a hand down the length of his face. "Ma, not you, too. I thought you were better than that."

"Son, I just want what's best for you."

"Then you'll accept Jariah and Ava into this family with open arms. She's the one, Ma, and I'm not going to lose her. Not for anything."

"Nicco, you can't be serious. She's Wesley's baby mother for goodness sake!"

"So what? They broke up almost a year ago, and she doesn't love him."

"But Wesley's your friend," she argued. "Sleeping with the mother of his child is…wrong."

Nicco cursed in Italian under his breath. "We went to the same high school and hit the clubs back in the day, but it's been years since we talked."

"I still don't like the idea of you dating his ex. There's something unnatural about it—"

"Ma, I'm a grown man. I can date whoever I want."

Mrs. Morretti opened her mouth to speak and then quickly closed it.

"You're so whipped, you can't think straight." Mr. Morretti stood, stalked over to the breakfast bar and scooped up the file folder beside the fruit bowl. "I had Gerald do a background check on Mrs. Brooks, and she isn't as squeaky clean as you think."

Nicco tried to conceal his anger, but inside he was seething with rage.

"Did you know that she's a registered member on over a half dozen dating sites?" He held the file up high in the air, waved it around, like a prosecutor wielding the proverbial smoking gun. "She's up to her neck in debt, so she's actively and aggressively looking for a rich, successful man to take care of her and her young daughter."

"Those profiles were created months ago, long before we ever met, and she deleted them weeks ago." Nicco picked up his plate, dumped his food into the garbage and put it in the sink. "Dad, there's nothing you can say to break us up, so save your breath."

"Read Gerald's report before making any hasty decisions."

"I don't need to. I know everything about Jariah that I need to know."

Mr. Morretti chucked the file on the kitchen table. "It's your life, do what you want, but don't come running to me when she screws you over."

Nicco wanted to lash out at his dad, but knew getting in a shouting match with Arturo would get him nowhere. Standing, he slipped on his sunglasses and took his car keys out of his pocket. "I'll see you guys later."

"Where are you going?" Mr. Morretti asked, glancing at his gold wristwatch. "We have to leave at eleven, and it's already ten fifteen. Are you packed and ready to go?"

Nicco frowned and scratched his head. "Packed and ready to go where?"

"To the airport. Our flight to Lisbon leaves at noon. We had discussed visiting Mr. Sarmento and scouting locations for our new offices, remember?"

"You mentioned it a few days ago, but you never confirmed the travel dates with me."

His eyes darkened three shades. "Mr. Sarmento was injured on *your* watch, but if you're too busy to visit one of my closest friends and associates, I'll go alone and apologize on your behalf."

"Where's Rafael? Why can't he go with you?"

"He flew to New York on the red eye. He had an urgent personal matter to deal with."

What personal matter? Rafael has no life! His brother was a workaholic with few hobbies and no close friends, so his hasty departure piqued Nicco's curiosity. Making a mental note to call him later, he said, "All right, Dad, I'll go with you to Lisbon."

Mr. Morretti sighed in relief. "I'm expecting you to come through for me in Lisbon, so stay focused. I don't have to tell you how important this visit is with Mr. Sarmento. He has been a client for years and pays big bucks for our services."

"Dad, I understand, but I can't stay in Portugal all week. I have a business meeting in L.A. on Friday that I can't afford to miss."

"Very well, we'll leave Thursday morning. I'll call First Officer Burke right now and…"

With a pang, Nicco realized he'd have to cancel his plans with Ava and Richie. The thought saddened him, but he forced a smile and dropped a kiss on his mother's cheek. "I'm going to go pack," he said, taking his cell phone out of his pocket. "See you guys in a bit."

Chapter 19

Jariah couldn't do it. Tried, but failed miserably. Typing a letter in Italian, and eavesdropping on her colleagues required extraordinary skill, and she was determined to finish the tasks on her checklist. She blocked out the noise in the reception area and continued working. Her coworkers were yakking it up like a bunch of tween girls at a slumber party, and as usual Jariah felt excluded.

Hearing her name, she narrowed her eyes and inclined her head toward the door. Raucous laughter seeped through the stark-white walls. Jariah knew her colleagues were talking trash about her, but instead of storming out of her office and giving the trio a tongue lashing, she kept her eyes on her computer screen.

Thoughts of Nicco overwhelmed her mind. She couldn't go five minutes without thinking of him, and spent hours on end looking at the pictures of him on her cell phone. It had been four days since his parents' anniversary bash, and although she'd stressed and fretted about leaving the party, nothing had changed between them. Nicco was still as sweet and as romantic as ever.

On Sunday, he'd surprised her with two dozen roses;

the following day he arranged for dinner to be delivered to her house from The Greek Isles, and last night on the phone he'd recited her favorite Maya Angelou poem to her. After days of sexting and flirting on Skype, Jariah was desperate to be back in his arms. Work was boring without Nicco to talk and laugh with, and every time she turned around Mrs. Reddick was breathing down her neck.

A message popped up on the corner of the screen. Jariah read the sentence, minimized her document and clicked on the internet icon. Nothing was more important than talking to Nicco, and Jariah was so anxious to see him she couldn't log into her Skype account fast enough. The moment his face filled the screen, her spirits lifted.

"You're looking gorgeous as usual. I love that shade of purple on you." Flashing a boyish smile, one that made his eyes twinkle, he slowly licked his lips. "Stand up so I can see the rest of your dress, or better yet, take it off so I can see what's *underneath* it."

"You wish!" Jariah couldn't keep a straight face and burst out laughing.

"That's right, baby, I do. I miss you bad, girl."

"You've only been gone for few days."

"I know, but it feels like years since I saw you. Don't you miss me? Even a little?" he asked, wearing a puppy-dog frown.

Jariah wanted to lie, to tell Nicco that he was being silly, but her conscience wouldn't let her. She longed to see him, to kiss and caress him, and was counting down the days until he returned from Lisbon. But she didn't want Nicco to know the truth, so she downplayed how she felt. "Of course I miss you. There's no one to bring me breakfast in bed or to rub my feet at the end of the day."

An amused expression covered his handsome face. "That's not *all* I'd like to rub."

That makes two of us, she thought, marveling at how

delicious he looked in his white button-down shirt and dark slacks.

"I hope you don't have plans tonight, because I'm making you a home-cooked meal."

Jariah raised an eyebrow. "That's going to be mighty hard to do from Portugal."

"I'll be back in Miami by eight."

"Tonight? But you're supposed to be heading straight from Lisbon to L.A."

"That was the plan, but I'm going crazy without you. I *have* to see you."

"So you're going to fly home for six hours, then fly back out? That's insane!"

"Not to me. As long as I can hold you in my arms, and kiss your beautiful face the trip will be worth it." He grinned, and his eyes lit up like a star. "I died laughing when I heard the message Ava left for me this morning. She is hilarious!"

The memory of her daughter singing her favorite pop song on Nicco's voice mail forced Jariah to laugh, as well. "That was very sweet of you to send Ava a gift box from Lisbon. She loved the souvenirs, devoured the chocolate seashells in one sitting and danced around the house for hours in her new Taylor Swift tour jacket!"

"I just wanted Ava to know that I was thinking about her, too."

And I love you for that.

"How are things going in Lisbon?" Jariah noted the dark lines under his eyes and wondered if he'd had a good night's sleep since arriving in Portugal four days earlier. "Did you visit with Mr. Sarmento yesterday?"

"Yeah, he was real happy to see us, and was even able to tell us more about the gunman."

"Did you finally close the deal with Sea Freight Shipping?" she asked.

"No. They're playing hard ball, so we rescinded our offer and shut down talks."

"I'm sorry to hear that. Are you disappointed?"

Nicco shrugged a shoulder and raked a hand through his hair. "Not really. There's plenty of money to be made in Lisbon, and Sea Freight Shipping is just one of many companies trying to break into the international market," he explained, loosening the knot in his burgundy tie. "On the upside, I found the perfect location for Dolce Vita Lisbon."

"That's great, baby. Congratulations! I'm so happy for you."

"We should celebrate at The Four Seasons," he proposed. "We can have dinner on the terrace and slow dance under the stars."

"That sounds wonderful Nicco, especially the part about us slow dancing."

"I thought you might like that." His gaze was full of longing and heat. "And when we get to the penthouse suite, I'm going to show you *just* how much I missed you."

Jariah was so excited she feared her heart would burst right out of her chest, but she faked a scowl and pretended to be upset. "Do you ever think of anything besides sex?"

"Yes, you, and when I'm not thinking about you, I'm dreaming about you."

Licking her lips, she fanned her hands to her face. *God help me.*

"I can't wait to see you," he said, leaning forward in his chair. "We might have to forgo dinner and spend the entire night in bed. Sound good to you?"

"Quit flirting and get off the phone." She blushed. "You have a plane to catch, and I'll kill you if you miss that flight!"

Chuckling, he threw his hands in the air like a crook surrendering to the police. "All right, all right, I'm leaving, take it easy, baby. I'll call you when I land at Miami International…"

Jariah heard a knock on the door, and reluctantly tore her gaze away from the computer screen. Fear knotted inside her chest, and panic gripped her heart. Standing in the doorway, wearing a fitted red business suit and a dark hostile glare was Vivica Morretti.

"Baby, what's wrong? Is everything okay?"

"Yes, of course," she lied, regaining the use of her mouth. "Have a safe flight."

Quickly, Jariah logged out of Skype and closed her monthly planner. She couldn't risk Mrs. Morretti seeing the love notes Nicco had given her, so she dropped it in her bottom drawer and jumped to her feet. Her stomach was twisted in knots, but she didn't let her fear show. If she did, Nicco's mother would eat her alive. "It's wonderful seeing you again, Mrs. Morretti. How are you?"

"Was that my son?" she asked, pointing at the computer. "He called you from Lisbon?"

"Yes, of course, we were talking about work, and—"

"Sex, right?"

A gasp fell from Jariah's lips.

"You used sex to entice and seduce my son, but I'm here to tell you the jig is up."

The temperature in the office shot through the roof.

"I know all about how you trapped Wesley Covington by willfully getting pregnant." Her tone was matter-of-fact, and her voice was patronizing. "You have several online dating profiles. I wouldn't be surprised if my son was just one of many wealthy, influential men supporting you."

"Is that what you think? That I'm after Nicco's money?"

"I don't think, Ms. Brooks. I know."

"If Nicco lost everything tomorrow, it wouldn't change how I feel about him. I love him because of who he is, not because of what he has. He's the man for me, and I plan to be in his life for many years to come."

"I have a hair appointment at noon, so I'm going to get right to the point." Mrs. Morretti flicked her thick, auburn locks over her shoulders. The former Broadway actress had a slender frame, a perfectly sculptured nose and radiant brown skin. She didn't have a crease or wrinkle in sight, and carried herself with the grace of a prima ballerina. "As of four o'clock today, you no longer work for Morretti Incorporated. You are not the right fit for this company or my son, and I expect you out of here by the end of the workday."

"With all due respect, you didn't hire me, and I don't work for you."

Her eyes were sharp, lethal daggers. "I'm a company stakeholder, and also one of the founding members. I have the power to make decisions just like anyone else on the board."

The news came as a shock and sent Jariah's heartbeat into an erratic tailspin. It took everything she had not to cry, and supreme effort not to argue. Mrs. Morretti spoke in a polite, quiet manner, and never once raised her voice. But her hatred was evident, as clear as the clouds in the morning sky.

Mrs. Morretti opened her Louis Vuitton purse and took out a white envelope. "Here's your termination letter and your severance pay," she said. "I understand the plight of single mothers, so I ensured that your settlement was more than generous."

A sickening wave of nausea bubbled up inside Jariah's throat. She didn't care what was inside the envelope, and dropped it on the desk.

"Open it," she instructed.

With her heart in her throat, Jariah took the envelope, ripped it open and cast a critical eye over the termination contract. It was a standard letter, legally binding, and there was nothing she could do to fight it. Staring at the check, she was sure the accounting department had made another mistake. Then, it hit her. *Is this severance pay or a bribe?* Jariah did the math in her head, and knew without a doubt that it was the latter.

"You have your money, so be on your way." Her features darkened, and her tone was sharp. "I'm not going to warn you again, Mrs. Brooks. Stay away from Nicco or you'll be sorry."

"Are you threatening me?"

"Keep your money-hungry paws off my son," she spat, "and concentrate on raising your daughter. She doesn't need a rich new stepfather."

Her words were a slap in the face. "I'm a good mother."

"That's not what I heard."

Anger surged through Jariah's veins. "You don't know anything about me—"

"Oh, yes, I do. You're as devious and as calculating as Nicco's last assistant, and I'm not going to sit back and let you hurt my son. He deserves the best, and you my dear, are not it."

Her vision blurred, grew thick with unshed tears, but through the haze Jariah saw Mrs. Morretti spin around and storm out of the office. In her mind, she replayed their conversation, and the more she thought about it, the more depressed she felt.

Wiping her eyes, she took a long, hard look at her severance check. Twenty-five thousand dollars was nothing to laugh at. It was enough to buy a new car and put a down payment on a house with a big backyard for Ava. And there would be some left over for a rainy day.

And you're going to need it, her conscience pointed out, *because as of four o'clock today you won't have a job...or a man.*

Chapter 20

"Welcome home, boss." Gerald opened the back door of the white stretch Hummer parked along the curb at Miami International Airport. "It's good to see you."

"Thanks, Gerald. Sorry for delay. I got held up in customs."

Exhausted, Nicco slid inside the car and dropped his brown leather briefcase at his feet.

Back behind the wheel, Gerald checked his rearview mirror and joined the slow-moving traffic on Airport Road. The walkways were clogged with travelers hailing taxicabs, dragging luggage and yapping on their cell phones. "How was your flight?"

"Terrible." Nicco unbuttoned his suit jacket and loosened the knot in his pinstripe tie. "Reminded me to never fly commercial again. Everyone in first-class was a mess!"

"It couldn't have been that bad."

"The turbulence was horrendous, and the soap star sitting beside me kept cooing in my ear and rubbing her fake boobs against my shoulder."

"You're right. It sounds horrible." Gerald chuckled and

tossed a glance over his right shoulder. "Six months ago you would have taken her to the lavatory for a quickie."

"I was stupid and reckless back then."

"And now?"

And now, I'm anxious to marry Jariah and start a family. The thought caused his chest to swell with pride. He'd been enamored with her from the day they'd met, and over the summer his feelings had developed into the real thing. With Jariah, he knew exactly where he stood, and never second-guessed her feelings. She proved her love and devotion to him every day, and always put their relationship first. He loved that about her, and knew without a doubt that she'd never betray his trust.

"Where to, boss?"

"Morretti Inc.," Nicco said, surfacing from his thoughts. Fatigued by the fourteen-hour flight from Lisbon, he settled into his seat and closed his tired eyes. "I have to pick up some files for my trip to L.A. tomorrow, but I won't be at the office long, so stay close by."

Rock music and the scent of seawater flooded the car through the open sunroof. Stars glimmered in the sky, fashionably dressed couples streamed in and out of upscale restaurants and nightclubs, and police officers mounted on horseback patrolled the crowded downtown streets.

Nicco spotted a girl with pigtails playing hopscotch in front of Dairy Queen and broke into a broad grin. Images of Ava filled his mind. The young girl had grabbed a hold of his heart from the onset and had been squeezing it ever since. Thinking about the afternoon he'd taken Ava and Richie to play miniature golf at Boomers made Nicco chuckle to himself.

"I think my mom has a crush on you," Ava had announced.

"What makes you so sure?"

"I heard her talking outside to our next-door neighbors, Sadie and Felicia, and she had a lot to say about you."

"Really?" he'd questioned, his curiosity getting the best of him. "What did she say?"

Ava had stuck out her left hand and wiggled her fingers. "It's gonna cost you."

Like a fool, he'd opened his wallet and took out ten dollars.

"Really? That's the best you can do? If you want me to spill the beans, you're going to have to do *much* better than that."

"Yeah," Richie had agreed. "Dig deep, Uncle Nicco! We need that money to buy candy!"

An hour later, Nicco was fifty dollars poorer, but felt ten feet tall. The next day, on his way home from work, he'd dropped by Tiffany & Co. and bought the most expensive engagement ring in the store. Nicco patted the front of his suit pocket to ensure the diamond solitaire was still safe and sound. He was ready to spend the rest of his life with Jariah and couldn't wait to see the look on her face when he popped the question at dinner later that evening. He didn't want to live without her, couldn't do it, and would be proud to call Ava his stepdaughter.

Nicco heard his cell phone ring and retrieved it from his briefcase. He slid his index finger across the screen and put his iPhone to his ear. "Nicco Morretti."

"This is Detective Katsu from the Miami Police Department," said a gruff voice. "We found your Mercedes. It's on fire."

Ice spread through Nicco's veins. At a loss for words, his thoughts spun out-of-control. He slumped against his seat, stunned and confused by the news. Panic and fear drenched his body in a cold, chilling sweat. Why hadn't Jariah called? Was she hurt? Was Ava okay?

"Do you know a woman by the name of Jariah Brooks?"

Nicco blinked, came to his senses. "Yes, of course," he said, raking a hand through his hair. "What happened? Where is she? Can I speak to her?"

"I'd rather not talk over the phone. Can you meet me at Ms. Brooks's residence? I'm in the process of taking her fiancé's statement and—"

"Fiancé!" Nicco shouted, his pulse pounding erratically in his ears. "What fiancé?"

There was a profound silence, and the distant wail of a police siren.

"When I arrived on the scene Ms. Brooks was standing outside of her residence with a man by the name of Wesley Covington," the detective explained. "He identified himself as her fiancé, led her back inside the house, and hasn't left her side since."

Slow, sensuous music penetrated Jariah's consciousness, but the stench of burnt rubber and smoke killed the romantic mood. Moistening her lips with her tongue, she opened her eyes, fully expecting to see Nicco lying beside her. He wasn't, but Wesley was.

All at once, everything came rushing back—her heated argument with Mrs. Morretti that morning, returning home to an empty house, primping and prepping for her late-night date with Nicco. Less than an hour later, Wesley and her neighbor Mr. Regula were banging on her door, imploring her to get out of the house. Outside, Nicco's Mercedes Benz S350 was engulfed in flames, and her complex was jam-packed with news trucks, fire engines and police cars. Jariah had never seen anything like it, and hours later, she still couldn't believe someone had brazenly set a car on fire in a neighborhood overrun with small children and young families.

Jariah yawned and rubbed the sleep from her eyes. She must have dozed off, because her head was on Wesley's chest, and his arms were wrapped around her shoulders.

Straightening, she noticed he was watching music videos and playing Scrabble on his iPhone. Once the police had taken her statement and left the house following a brief look around, they'd sat on the living-room couch and had a blunt conversation. Her first question? Whether or not he'd sent that bogus email message to her parents. He'd coughed like a smoker on his death bed and then fervently denied being involved. Jariah didn't believe him, but decided to put the whole ugly incident behind her. Her parents were back in her life, and that was all that mattered to Jariah.

"How was your nap? Feeling better?"

"A little." Knowing she looked a mess, she straightened her sundress and combed a hand through her curly disheveled hair. "Thanks for sticking around, Wesley. If not for you, the police would have hauled me to jail and thrown away the key."

"I'm glad I could help." He moved closer and draped an arm around her shoulder. "Jariah, you mean the world to me, and I've never stopped loving you."

Biting the inside of her cheek, she glanced away from his piercing gaze.

"I'm ready to step up to the plate, and to be the man you need me to be." His voice was filled with sincerity. He placed a hand on her thigh. "I almost lost you tonight, and I don't want to lose you again."

"That's too bad. You're too late."

At the sound of Nicco's curt, brisk voice, Jariah felt a turbulent rush of panic. By now, he knew about his car, and the fire that had destroyed it. Inwardly, she feared he'd blow up at her or blame her for what happened, and that had her on edge. Taking in a deep breath, Jariah stood and prepared to learn her fate.

"You've said you're peace. Now leave."

Wesley surged to his feet. "Make me." His nostrils flared and his jaw clenched.

Nicco wanted to sock in the man in the face, but he didn't want the police, who were standing outside in the parking lot, to arrest him for assault. He couldn't stomach seeing Jariah with her ex, so he crossed the room and draped a hand around her waist. "I need to talk to my girlfriend alone, so you can show yourself out."

"You're never going to last," he sneered, a scowl staining his lips. "When you get sick of playing second fiddle to his career, and all of his *other* women, give me a call."

Nicco chided himself to keep his temper in check, but the moment he heard the front door slam he exploded in anger. "What the hell is going on?" he demanded, dropping his hands from around her waist. "Are you out of your damn mind?"

Jariah tried to touch him, but Nicco stepped back, out of reach. "Baby, I am so sorry about your car, but I swear, I had nothing to do with the fire—"

"I don't give a shit about the Mercedes."

"Then why are you so mad? Why are you shouting?"

"Because I flew over four thousand miles to see you, only to find you hugged up on the couch with your no-good ex," he growled through clenched teeth. "Why was Wesley here? And don't tell me he came to see Ava, because I called your parents after I got off the phone with Detective Katsu, and they told me she's spending the weekend with them."

"Wesley had a bad day at work, and needed someone to talk to."

"Then he should call a shrink, not you."

"Nicco, we dated for five years, and we have a child together—"

"I don't like seeing him here."

"Too bad," she snapped, growing frustrated with his attitude. "He's Ava's father."

"Yeah, he's Ava's father, *not* your man, so remember that the next time he's rubbing your knee and whispering bullshit lines in your ear."

Nicco saw her face harden like stone and knew he'd crossed the line. In three short strides, he was at her side, pulling her to his chest. Slowly and tenderly, he stroked her hair and neck. "Damn, I'm sorry. I shouldn't have said that."

"You're right. You shouldn't have. You're acting like a jealous lover, and you have no reason to be. I've never given you a reason to doubt my love and fidelity, and I never will."

"I know, but I can't help it. I lose my head whenever I see you with another guy."

Jariah poked him in the chest. "Now you know how I felt when Estelle tried to jump your bones!"

"Baby, you're the only woman I want. You know that."

His gaze met hers, weakening the hard, impenetrable shell around her heart.

"Did you see the person who set the fire?"

Jariah shook her head and wore an apologetic smile. "No, unfortunately, I didn't. I was upstairs in the shower, and the next thing I know, Wesley and my neighbor Mr. Regula were banging on the front door, yelling at me to get out of the house."

"You must have been terrified."

"Yeah, mostly of them breaking in and finding me in my birthday suit!"

The thought of her naked, curvy body glistening with

water sent a shiver down his spine. Nicco wanted to make love to Jariah more than anything, but didn't act on his impulse. It wasn't the right time. Not with cops, firefighters and reporters roaming around her complex.

"It wasn't as dramatic as it sounds." Jariah snuggled against him. "By the time I got dressed and went outside the firefighters had the fire contained, and the police were interviewing witnesses."

"I spoke to the lead detective on the case, and he had a lot of interesting information to share," Nicco said as his gaze drifted to the front window. "I'm going to call a family meeting next week so Detective Katsu can bring everyone up to speed."

"But you're leaving for L.A. tomorrow and won't be back for two weeks."

"Once I learned about the fire, I called the VP of the Childs Corporation and rescheduled our meeting for October." Nicco gave her a serious no-nonsense look. "And this time you're coming with me. No excuses."

"I'm there. Spending time with you at a world-famous resort sounds like heaven."

Wrapping her up in his arms, he lifted her chin and covered her mouth with a deep, passionate kiss. "I'm going outside to wait for the tow truck, and you're going upstairs to pack an overnight bag. I'm taking you back to my place."

"But your parents are staying with you."

"Baby, my estate is over fifteen thousand square feet, and they have their own private wing," he said, patting her affectionately on the hips. "Besides, they'll be too busy watching, *Italia's Got Talent* to pay us any mind!"

As Jariah reflected on her conversation with Nicco's mother she felt a nervous flutter in her belly. Her head throbbed, and her heart ached at the memory of Vivica's viscous words. *You're devious, and calculating... My son deserves the best, and, you're not it.* The thought of being without Nicco—of not seeing him or hearing his voice or feeling the warmth of his touch—was killing her inside. But she'd rather lose him than put a wedge between him and his parents. He'd find love with someone else, and she had Ava, and a healthy, renewed relationship with her mom and dad to be thankful for.

You deserve to have it all, whispered her inner voice.

Encouraged by her thoughts, she swallowed the lump in her throat and told Nicco about her unexpected visit that morning from his mom. "After she fired me, she made it very clear that I'm not good enough for you, and that she'll never welcome me or Ava into your family."

"To be honest, I'm not surprised. Ma's always been overprotective, and it takes her a while for her warm up to people, *especially* women dating her sons." Nicco gave Jariah a peck on the cheek and told her not to worry. "Ma will come around. I know it."

"That's it? That's all you have to say?" Incredulous, Jariah folded her arms across her chest and gave him a pointed look. "I've been a basket case all day, and all you can say is, 'Ma will come around'?"

His grin, though tinged with amusement, didn't cheer her. And neither did the hand he placed on her shoulder. "Leave Ma to me. I can handle her."

"Fine, but until you do, I won't be sleeping at your place or traveling out of town with you."

"Really?"

"I'm afraid so," she said.

"You leave me no choice then." Nicco whipped his iPhone out of his pocket, punched in a number and put it to his ear. "Hello, yes, this is Nicco Morretti... I'd like to book the penthouse suite for the rest of the week..."

Moments later, he ended the call and pointed at the staircase. "Go pack and hurry up or there'll be hell to pay when we get to The Four Seasons."

Jariah shot him a lusty smile. "Promise?"

Chapter 21

"Now that everyone's here, and the kids ran off to play, let's get down to business."

Everyone gathered inside the living room in Nicco's Coral Gables mansion turned toward the two, gray-haired detectives standing beside the fireplace. To calm her nerves, Jariah snuggled closer to Nicco, drawing comfort from his touch. Designer fragrances and the spicy aromas drifting out of the kitchen created a delicious scent. Chef Gambo and his team were preparing a feast, and every few minutes Jariah heard the flamboyant chef shouting instructions in Italian. Laughter penetrated the windows and the sound of Ava's and Richie's high-pitched giggles lightened the bleak mood.

Sitting beside Nicco on the couch should have quieted her troubled mind, but Jariah couldn't stop thinking about what happened on Friday night. Three days had passed since the fire, and although the police had cleared her as a suspect, she knew it would take a lot longer than seventy-two hours to win over Arturo and Vivica Morretti.

Her thoughts wandered to last night. At dinner, she'd sensed the couple's displeasure, their unhappiness, and if it were not for Ava sitting beside her eating happily, she would have left the five-star restaurant and returned home. Nicco insisted that things would get better in time, but Jariah suspected his parents would never accept her.

Casting her gaze around the spacious, sun-drenched room, she marveled at just how good-looking the Morretti men were. It didn't seem fair that they were all attractive, successful and filthy rich. Demetri, a baseball superstar with dreamy eyes and a chiseled physique was soft-spoken, great with kids and wholly devoted to his fiancée, Angela Kelly. The couple sat cuddled up on the sofa, his arm draped around her shoulders, and they shared kisses when they thought no one was looking. Rafael, the firstborn and heir to the Morretti shipping empire, had a somber disposition but on the rare occasion that he smiled, he could give any Hollywood heartthrob a serious run for their money.

"We've interviewed several witnesses, and have generated some strong leads, but we still have a lot of holes in our investigation," Detective Katsu explained. "We were hoping you could fill in some of the holes for us."

"What do you want to know?" Arturo glanced between the detectives. "I have nothing to hide and I want the bastard responsible for the fire brought to justice."

Detective Katsu took a pen out of his shirt pocket and flipped open his blue spiral notebook. "I'd like to start with Demetri," he announced. "Why did you file a restraining order against your former publicist, Nichola Caruso?"

"Because she kept dropping by my estate unannounced. My lawyer said filing a restraining order would be in my best interest, so I filed the paper work with the court last week."

"I've seen this happen a million times." Detective Bueschler stroked his broad chin, regarded Demetri closely. "You had a fling with Ms. Caruso that went south, didn't you?"

"Our relationship was strictly platonic. Nothing inappropriate ever happened. Nichola was like a kid sister to me, and I viewed her as nothing more than a great friend."

Detective Katsu nodded, and then flipped to the next page in his notebook. "Why did Tye Caldwell resign from Morretti Incorporated? Was the decision of his own free will?"

Jariah felt Nicco's body tense and she squeezed his right hand to offer her support. His shoulders stiffened, and the veins in his neck were twitching, but his voice didn't betray his emotions. "It was a mutual decision between all parties involved."

Detective Bueschler barked a cold, bitter laugh. "Mr. Caldwell's Facebook and Twitter posts tell a *very* different story. He hates your family, and it sounds like he's out for revenge."

"Tye would never do anything to hurt us," Nicco argued, rising from his seat.

"I can't prove it, but I have a feeling my former assistant, Gracie O'Conner, is involved."

"That petite brunette with the braces?" Detective Bueschler doubled over, chuckled as if he was at a comedy club. "Right!"

"Tye didn't vandalize my restaurant, and he damn sure didn't set my car on fire. He isn't even in Miami. He's been backpacking in Europe for months."

"So you've been in contact with him then?"

"No," Nicco said in an exasperated tone of voice, "but my security team monitors his movements, and his ex-wife does a great job of keeping me in the loop."

Detective Katsu closed his notebook. "If Tye's out of the country, then we're back to square one, because I thought for sure he was our guy."

"Arturo, can you think of anyone who would want to

harm you and your family?" Detective Bueschler asked, stroking the length of his jaw. "Anyone at all?"

Rafael gave a wry laugh. "Pull up a seat detectives. This could take a while."

Eyebrows raised, the detectives exchanged a curious look.

Silence plagued the living room, causing the tension in the air to rise.

"Non voglio farti del male, Nicco, ma questo deve essere detto," Mrs. Morretti said, her voice matter-of-fact. *"Jariah ha datato un sacco di uomini. Come fai a sapere uno dei suoi amanti online non ha definito le Mercedes in fiamme in una rabbia gelosa..."*

A crippling pain racked Jariah's body. Tears pricked her eyes, and it hurt to swallow. She couldn't believe what she was hearing, couldn't believe the lies coming out of Mrs. Morretti's mouth. *You think one of my online boyfriends set Nicco's car on fire in a jealous rage? What online boyfriends? I don't have time to play the field; I'm a single mother, and my daughter is my number one priority!* Something inside Jariah snapped, causing her pulse to go haywire, and her temperature to spike. Her fast, heavy breathing filled the air, and her heart was beating so loud she knew everyone inside the living room could hear it.

Straightening her spine, she pinned back her shoulders and openly glared at Mrs. Morretti. Her stomach muscles clenched and contracted, but she spoke in a clear, confident voice. *"Perché, Nicco è l'unico uomo che io sono uscito e stato intimo con da quando ho rotto con il mio ex. Non ci sono gelosi ex-fidanzati, e non ho alcuna intenzione di datazione chiunque altro. Nicco è tutto l'uomo che mi serve, e non ho mai amato nessuno più di quanto ami tuo figlio."*

To Jariah's surprise, Vivica cooed, Demetri and Rafael

wore matching ear-to-ear grins and Mr. Morretti nodded his head in approval.

"Y-y-you speak Italian," Mrs. Morretti stammered, her face as pale as her white, cashmere scarf. "I had no idea... That means you understood what I said last night at dinner."

"Sì, l'ho fatto, ma io non ho intenzione di lasciare che tu o chiunque vieni tra me e l'uomo che amo. Nicco è la mia anima gemella, e non sarò mai lasciare la sua parte."

"Baby, that's beautiful." Nicco's tone was soft, a soothing caress, and happiness shone in his eyes. "I love you, too, more than you will ever know."

His words comforted Jariah, made her feel incredibly special, but she turned to Detective Katsu and asked the question on the tip of her tongue. "Is it safe for me to go home? The Sheraton is great, but I'm sick of eating room service, and my daughter misses her friends."

"Absolutely not. The lunatic who started that fire is still out there," Nicco said, furiously shaking his head. "You and Ava will move in here for the time being."

"We're going to stay here? Yahoo!" Ava raced into the living room with Richie in tow.

"I appreciate your very generous offer, but we can't live here. I don't want to set the wrong example for my daughter."

"The wrong example?" Nicco repeated, folding his arms. "What are you saying?"

"That I won't shack up with you. I made that mistake once, and I won't do it again."

Their eyes aligned, and an awkward silence fell over the room.

"Then," Nicco said, with a grin, "I guess this is the perfect time, Ava."

"For what?" Richie stopped and scratched his head.

Jariah shot Nicco a what-are-you-talking-about gaze.

And she watched him reach into his pocket and pull out a small turquoise box. He presented it to Ava, and she burst out laughing.

"Nicco, I can't marry you," she said, cupping a hand over her mouth to stifle her giggles. "I'm only six, and you're *super* old!"

Everyone smiled and chuckled.

"Ava, I bought this ring for you as a sign of my love," Nicco said.

"Wow, it's pretty." Ava snatched the heart-shaped diamond out of the box and slid it on her finger. "Thank you, Nicco. I'll never take it off. Not even when I go to bed!"

"I promise to take care of you, and to do everything I can to make you happy."

Glancing around, Ava shielded her mouth with the back of her hand. "Are you going to help me do my homework and sneak me chocolate cookies when my mom's not looking?"

Nicco winked. "Yup, *and* I'll take you to Chuck E. Cheese's on Fridays so you can beat Richie at 'Western Wrangler.'"

"Yahoo!" Ava threw her arms around Nicco's neck, and kissed him on the cheek. "And I promise to be the best stepdaughter ever!"

"Is it okay if I propose to your mom now?" Nicco asked. "Is that okay with you?"

Nodding, Ava scooted behind Jariah and shoved her into his open arms.

"Mom, it's your turn!" she said excitedly. "I think Nicco has a ring for you, too!"

Tears flowed freely down Jariah's cheeks, and the living room became a big, white blur. Her heart was pounding, and her breathing was so shallow she feared her next breath could be her last.

"Baby, I can't imagine my life without you in it. You're

smart, vivacious and fiesty as hell, and knowing you has made me a better man."

Jariah sniffed, willed herself not to sob. There was nothing cute about her cry, and she didn't want to ruin the moment by slobbering all over herself.

"You are the best thing that has ever happened to me, and I want to spend the rest of my life with you." Nicco took her hand, and pressed it flat against his chest. "You're my life, my oxygen, the very air I breathe, and I want you to marry you more than anything in the world."

It was the biggest surprise of Jariah's life, a moment she would never forget, and she couldn't contain the excitement bubbling up inside her. *"Ti amo così tanto! Certo che ti sposo! Tu sei tutto quello che potevo desiderare in un uomo e molto di più!"*

"Baby, you're jumping the gun," Nicco whispered. "Say yes *after* I propose."

Jariah giggled, felt happier than she'd ever been. Out of the corner of her eye, she spotted Mrs. Morretti dabbing her cheeks with a pink hankerchief and wondered if she was crying tears of joy or grief. Deciding it didn't matter, Jariah returned her gaze to the man she loved, her heart so full of love and affection she felt like she was going to burst.

Nicco took another turquoise box out of his back pocket.

"Dang, bro, just how big *is* your pocket? What are you going to pull out next? A brand-new car!" Rafael laughed at his own joke. But when Nicco dropped to one knee and clasped Jariah's left hand, he was the first one to whip out his iPhone and start snapping pictures.

"Jariah Brooks, will you marry me?"

The engagement ring was a stunner, a rose-gold sparkler that twinkled and shined, but it was the loving expression on Nicco's face that took Jariah's breath away. They had a lot of obstacles to contend with, and his mother would probably never accept her into the family, but Jariah chose to focus on the positives. As long as she had Nicco's unconditional love and support nothing else mattered.

Jariah wanted to dive into Nicco's arms and plant a sexy, red-hot kiss on him, but decided to have a little fun with him first. "I don't know. I'm, ah, having second thoughts."

His face fell, and the grin slid off his mouth. "You are?"

"The ring is *so* big, and look at all the sparkling baugette diamonds. It's *so* not me."

Nicco tossed his head back and erupted in laughter. Chuckling, he scooped Jariah up in his arms and spun her around until she begged in English *and* Italian for him to stop. "That's what you get for teasing me. I almost had a heart attack!"

Laughing, cheering and applauding, the Morretti family surrounded the newly engaged couple, offering hugs, kisses and well-wishes.

"Welcome to the family." Arturo kissed Jariah on both cheeks and whispered in her ear, "You're the perfect woman for my son, and likely the only person who can keep him in check. I'm thrilled, and I can't wait for you guys to fill this big, empty mansion with children."

Me, too, Mr. Morretti. Me, too.

It was a beautiful moment, but Jariah wished her parents had been there to witness it.

Later, after Nicco's family left, they'd drive over to her mom and dad's house to share the wonderful news.

"Congratulations," Detective Katsu said. "We're leaving, but we'll be in touch."

"Thanks for stopping by." Nicco shook hands with the detectives. "Take care."

"Isn't it great? Now I have three grandmas instead of two!" Ava wrapped her arms around Mrs. Morretti. "I love you, Nicco's mom. You make the best peanut butter cookies ever!"

It was the first time Jariah had ever seen Mrs. Morretti smile, and when she bent down and kissed Ava's forehead Jariah wanted to weep for joy. "I know we got off to a rocky start, but I hope one day we can be friends," she said, choking back tears.

"I'd like that, and from now on please call me Vivica. You're going to marry my son, and one day give me grandchildren. Mrs. Morretti is *way* too formal!"

Jazz music flowed through the sound system, and waiters appeared holding trays filled with artichoke brushetta, crab beignets and rose champagne. Toasts were made, laughter abounded and the appetizers were devoured in the blink of an eye. Richie told knock-knock jokes with the skill of a seasoned comic, and Ava wowed everyone with her Taylor Swift impression.

Alone in the corner of the room, Nicco and Jariah kissed and laughed like teenagers inside a parked car at Lover's Lane. Boldly capturing her around the waist, he took her in his arms and tenderly stroked her cheeks with the back of his hand.

"You're the sexiest, most captivating woman I have ever seen, Mrs. Nicco Morretti-to-be." Nicco's mouth moved over her forehead and across her cheeks, teased and tickled her warm flesh. His lips continued to arouse and entice her, caused waves of pleasure to consume her body. "Think we should kick everyone out so we can have engagement sex?"

Jariah swatted his forearm. "Nicco, you're terrible. I swear sex is all you ever think about."

"Don't *Nicco* me. You were thinking the *exact* same thing."

A giggle fell out of her mouth. "You know me so well."

"Of course I do. We were made for each other."

Their eyes aligned, made an unspoken vow, a promise.

"You've made me a very happy man, Jariah." Nicco

bowed his head and murmured into her ear in a voice rife with hunger and need. "I love you, baby, always and forever."

"I love you with all my heart, Nicco, for as long as we both shall live."

Nicco kissed her eyelids, the tip of her nose, brushed his lips gently against her earlobes, and when their lips touched, Jariah knew all of her dreams had finally come true. He kissed her slowly, thoughtfully, like a man hopelessly in love, and his touch warmed her all over.

"I can't wait for you and Ava to move in," he said, burying his hands into her hair. "The three of us are going to have a blast together."

"And now that I'm unemployed, I'll have plenty of time to cook for you."

"Don't even try it. I expect you at the office bright and early Monday morning."

Jariah pouted, made a face. "Can I at least keep the severance check?"

"No, but if you're a good girl I'll let you drive the Lambo when we go see your parents."

"Wow," she gushed, widening her eyes. "You really *do* love me!"

They cracked up, and the warmth and beauty of their unbridled laughter made everyone around them smile.

* * * * *